DAVID ALMOND

SECRET HEART

Hodder
Children's
Books

A division of Hachette Children's Books

A Catalogue record for this book is available
from the British Library

ISBN-13: 978 0 340 94498 1

Typeset in Bembo by Avon DataSet Ltd, Bidford on Avon, Warwickshire

Printed and bound in Great Britain by Clays Ltd, St Ives plc

The paper and board used in this paperback by
Hodder Children's Books are natural recyclable products
made from wood grown in sustainable forests. The manufacturing
processes conform to the environmental regulations of
the country of origin.

Hodder Children's Books
a division of Hachette Children's Books
338 Euston Road, London NW1 3BH
An Hachette Livre UK company

About the author

David Almond's debut novel *Skellig* is one of the most remarkable children's novels published in recent years. It

Also by David Almond

Skellig
Kit's Wilderness
Heaven Eyes
Counting Stars
Wild Girl, Wild Boy – A Play
Skellig – A Play
The Fire-Eaters
Clay

Other titles published by Hodder Children's Books:

Red Moon
Pizza On Saturday
Rachel Anderson

Cherry Heaven
The Diary of Pelly D
L.J. Adlington

The Door of No Return
Sarah Mussi

For Maggie Noach

The tiger padded through the night. Joe Maloney smelt it, the hot, sour breath, the stench of its pelt. The odour crept through the streets, through his open window and into his dreams. He felt the animal wildness on his tongue, in his nostrils. The tiger moved as if it knew him, as if it was drawn to him. Joe heard its footpads on the stairs. He heard its long slow breath, the distant sighing in its lungs, the rattle in its throat. It came inside. It filled the bedroom. The huge head hung over him. The glittering cruel eyes stared into him. The hot tongue, harsh as sandpaper, licked his arm. The mouth was wide open, the curved teeth were poised to close on him. He prepared to die. Then someone somewhere called:

'Tiger! Tiger! Tiger! Tiger!'

And it was gone.

At the window he made a funnel of his hands and peered out. There it was, loping away beneath the orange streetlights on the pale pavement between the pale houses. Longer than a man, taller than a boy. 'Tiger!' he gasped, and it paused and swung its head to search him out. 'Tiger!' he whispered, as its eyes steadied and it gazed up at him.

'Tiger!' someone called, and he saw the man – a huge dark figure in the shadows of the Cut. 'Tiger!'

Before it turned again, the tiger watched the boy. Stars glittered in its eyes. It drew Joe Maloney into itself. Then it turned again and loped on towards the Cut. Hips and shoulders rocked. Tail swung. It returned to the dark figure waiting there, and they left his sight, left the village, went into the deeper night outside.

FRIDAY

One

All that night, Joe Maloney sweated, twisted and turned. He dreamed that engines roared and lights blazed. Men yelled, children screamed, dogs yelped. Metal hammered on metal. He dreamed that the surface of the earth was lifted and hung from great hooks in the sky. Beneath it, shapeless beasts danced in the dark. Then he lay dead still. Easy breath, easy heart. He smelt sawdust, canvas, animal sweat, animal dung. Gentle noises, creakings and flappings. He felt something fingering his skull, felt someone whispering his name. He was about to wake up in some new place.

'Joe!' yelled his mum. 'Joseph!'

He opened his eyes: just his bedroom, pale sunlight filtering through thin curtains, childhood drawings Sellotaped to the walls, his clothes in a heap on the floor. He sniffed the air, trying to smell the tiger again.

'Joe!' she called. 'Come on, son, will you?'

He slithered from the tangled bed, picked up his clothes and dressed himself. He dragged on his heavy boots. He sniffed, listened, narrowed his eyes.

'Joe!'

In the bathroom, he splashed water on to himself, then leaned close to the mirror, inspected his pale face, his tangled hair, his one green eye, his one brown eye. He touched his skin. He hadn't changed. He was still just Joe Maloney.

'Joseph!'

He went down into the kitchen. She was at the table, pouring orange juice. She shook her head and clicked her tongue. She tugged his shirt square on his shoulders. She fastened the laces of his boots. 'Joe Maloney. What you like?'

He grinned.

'L-like me,' he said.

She cuffed him gently on the shoulder.

'Like you. And you're going to need me to get you up and get you dressed all your life?'

He grinned again.

'Yes.'

He buttered some toast and chewed it. She smiled, and smoothed his hair with her fingers and palms.

'I had a d-dream,' Joe said.

'Now there's a change.'

'There was . . .'

She shook her head, but she leaned towards him, about to listen.

'There was . . .?' she said.

Joe rubbed his eyes and blinked. He looked out of the window and gasped. The summit of a blue tent stood high over the rooftops at the village's edge.

'What's that?'

'Eh?'

'L–look, Mum.'

He jabbed the air. A blue tent, a blue paler than the morning sky. A great blue tent that trembled slightly in the morning breeze.

'What?' she said.

'There, look, Mum.'

She narrowed her eyes and peered.

'Tent,' he said. 'A tent.'

'Oh . . . Aye. Now where might that come from?'

They gazed at it together, the slope of blue rising from the dusty red rooftops.

'Fancy that,' she said. 'A circus or something, eh? Last time a circus came to Helmouth was in . . .' She shrugged. 'Before our time, I reckon.'

Joe shoved a piece of toast into his mouth. She put her arm around him as he prepared to go out.

'Now, then, Joseph Maloney,' she said.

He lowered his eyes then turned them to her.

'You know what I'm going to say, don't you?'

'Yes, Mum.'

'You make sure you get into school today. OK?'

'OK, Mum.'

She kissed him.

'Don't want that rotten Wag Man coming round again, do I?'

'No, Mum.'

'You. What a lad. Sometimes wonder what I brought into the world. How can a lad be so lovely and so much trouble? Can you answer me that?'

'No, Mum.'

'No, Mum. Come on, then, give us a kiss.'

She took him to the door, watched him walk through the garden to the front gate. She raised her finger as he turned to wave. 'Be sure, now,' she said.

'Yes, Mum,' he said, then hurried towards the Cut.

Two

He rocked on his skinny legs. He dragged the heels of his ungainly boots. He hesitated, sighed, and gathered his strength before he moved through the Cut. Some of Cody's lot were already there, where it opened to the wasteland. Mac Bly, Geordie Carr, Jug Matthews, Goldie Wills, cigarettes fuming in their fists. Joe lowered his eyes as he passed through. They elbowed him, stuck out their feet to trip him.

'Only Maloney,' they sang softly, 'lalalalaaaaa!'

'Look. The freaks is come,' hissed Plug. He pointed at the tent.

'You'll feel at home today, Maloney.'

'Only Maloney, lalalalaaaaahahahaha!'

'You've got to try standing up to them,' his mother had said. But he didn't know how to look at them, never mind how to speak to them. He kept his head down as he made his way through.

He wiped the spit off his cheek with his cuff. He moved away from them across the wasteland, towards the great blue tent.

Their voices followed him: directed now at the circus.

'Clear off, scum! Clear off, Gyppo scum! Take your tent somewhere else! Ahhahahaha!'

More kids were on the wasteland, younger kids, singles and little groups, spread out in a broad circle, watching.

A massive poster was draped across the tent:

HACKENSCHMIDT'S CIRCUS
! THE FINAL TOUR !
! YOUR FINAL CHANCE !
! NEVER **to be seen** AGAIN !

Beyond the tent were ancient cars and trucks and caravans.

He heard his name spoken, turned to find Stanny Mole coming up behind him.

'Heard it coming in the night,' said Stanny. 'Thought there was a war or something starting.'

Joe nodded.

'But it's just a stupid old circus,' said Stanny. 'Come on, let's wag it.'

Joe thought of his mum and he shook his head.

'No,' he said. 'Got to go in today.'

But he didn't move. He looked at the tent and the wasteland beyond it and he knew this would be yet another day he didn't go to school.

A thin pale man in a goatee beard came out of the tent. A bunch of little dogs in silver skirts danced around him. He gave out leaflets that offered half-price tickets for the first night.

'Look at the state of him,' said Stanny. 'Look at the state of it all. Come on, Joe, eh?'

The man came towards the boys. He winked and reached out and poked Joe in the ribs.

'Hello, you,' he said.

He turned his mouth down to make a sad face then turned it up to make a happy face.

'Hello,' he said again.

He reached out to poke him again, but Stanny pulled Joe back.

'Leave him alone,' he said. 'Come *on*, Joe. Stop dreaming.'

They started to move away, but Joe stopped again.

There was a girl in the doorway of the tent. She was small and dark-haired, same age as the boys. She had a grubby mac on, fastened tightly at the waist, and black tights and silver slippers. She held the canvas to one side. Behind her the air in the tent was a dusky blue.

11

She met Joe's eyes and smiled and held the doorway further open.

Stanny spat.

'Come *on*,' he said. 'Let's wag it before anybody sees.'

'Aye . . . aye.'

'What you staring at?'

'Nothing.'

Joe couldn't take his eyes from her. He'd seen her before. He was sure he'd seen her before.

Stanny tugged his arm.

'She's just a Gyppo circus lass.'

Joe stood his ground.

'H-hang on,' he said.

Stanny tugged him harder.

'Come on, Joe. Come *on*, man.'

And Joe turned his eyes away, and headed downhill with Stanny, across the wasteland, away from Helmouth.

Three

Helmouth. It was called a village, but was just a place at the city's edge, before the wasteland started. A mess of new houses and old houses and cracked pavements and roads. The Stag's Head with graffiti sprayed on its walls. A boarded-up KwikSave. A Ladbrokes and The Chip Plaice and Kurl Up & Dye. The Booze Bin, where Joe's mother worked. They kept saying there'd be great things coming – a swimming-pool, a leisure centre, a shopping centre, a new estate. But it was like Helmouth had been left behind, like it had been forgotten about. Men had been seen there, looking through theodolites and marking the earth with posts and tape. Bulldozers once came and ripped the earth open and shoved it into heaps. But they all just went away again. Nothing happened. In Helmouth, everything just came to nothing.

As Joe and Stanny walked, larks kept rising. They dashed from the grass and spiralled into the sky. They hung there, nearly out of sight, singing and singing. Joe raised his head, gazed at them, heard them singing in the sky and singing in his heart.

'Listen,' he whispered.

'Joe,' said Stanny Mole.

'L–listen to them all, Stanny.'

He put his finger to his lips. Stanny spat.

'We're going away again this weekend. Me and Joff. You could come with us, Joe. Joe?'

But Joe's attention was lost in the sky.

'Joe!' Stanny said. 'I wonder why I bother with you. Joe!'

He yanked Joe's arm, pulled him from his dreams, walked on.

The land out here was filled with familiar names, names that had been passed down from children to children to children. They grew out of old stories, lethal games, awful discoveries. The Field of Skulls, the Ratty Paddocks, the Lostleg Railway, the Blood Pond, Adder Lane.

'Five o'clock tomorrow morning,' said Stanny. 'Come with us, Joe. Just imagine it.'

Joe stared to where Stanny pointed. A mile away, there was the motorway where the traffic droned in a haze of fumes and sunlight. Beyond it, the earth turned upward again, to the Silver Forest, the Golden Hills, the Black Bone Crags reaching to the sky.

'We'll walk all day,' Stanny said. 'Way past all this. We'll walk to where it's wild, really really wild. We'll have our combats on. Knives and catapults and snares in our pockets. We'll kill something for lunch. We'll strip a tree to make the shelter. We'll light a fire. Joff'll drink and talk about his army days and we'll listen to the night. There's nowt like it, Joe.'

'Aye?'

'You've never been there, have you?'

'No.'

It was true. He'd never been. But he often walked as far as the motorway and gazed through the noise and the traffic to the enticing land beyond. And he often walked there in his dreams. Sometimes he walked in his dreams with Stanny through the Silver Forest. Sometimes he walked with his mum. More and more often, he walked with a stranger, a girl. He could never see her clearly, but she walked quickly and eagerly at his side.

'And you've never even been away from home for a whole night,' said Stanny. 'Have you?'

Joe shook his head. Never.

'Well, then. 'Bout time you started. You've got to start toughening up, Joe. You've got to . . .'

Stanny spat and cursed. Joe was staring towards the distant densely packed trees, to the tracks like pencil lines heading for the hilltops, to the purple heather and the black rocks and the streams like threads of silver. He tilted his head, narrowed his eyes, gazed into the sky. And there they were, the creatures he'd known since he was small, the beasts that wheeled in the empty air above the Black Bone Crags. He turned to his friend, saw that Stanny saw nothing. He kicked the earth. The words he spoke stumbled on his tongue.

'Wh-why d'you want to go there with J-Joff?' he said.

'Joff? You come and you'll see.'

'Once we s-said we'd go out there together. Just you and—'

'That was ages back. We were kids. We did nowt about it.' He glared. 'And some of us grew up, Joe.'

He picked up two fist-sized stones and started lifting them up and down towards his shoulders. He shoved them into Joe's hands.

'Look, you do it. Get your muscles working.'

They flopped from Joe's hands back to the ground.

'What you like?' said Stanny.

He turned away. He spat.

'Come with me and Joff. He'll make a man of you.'

Joe stared at the horizon again. Even though he couldn't name them, he saw what flew there in the day. He knew what prowled on the earth there in his dreams. He walked on, and shivered at the thought of going there with Joff.

Four

Joff. Redness in the whites of his eyes, snakeskin tattoo around his throat, two gold teeth, shaved head, muscles. Once at Stanny's house, Joe saw him stick a safety-pin through the flesh on his forearm and close the clasp. He grinned. Then he got another pin and stuck it in his other arm and grinned again. Stanny said there were other things he did, other ways of showing that pain was nothing. He knew how to spit paraffin out of his mouth and breathe fire. He knew how to hold his breath under water till you were sure he must die. He was tough. He knew how to survive. If Joe spent some time with him he'd see it all, he'd learn it all.

One afternoon Joe had come home and Joff was at the kitchen door, leaning on the frame, one foot on the step. He caught Joe in his arms as he came around the corner of the house and lifted him to his chest.

'Hello, son,' he said, and Joe caught his fiery smoky

breath. 'Nice time at school, then?'

Joff let him go. Joe hurried in to his mum, who stood against the kitchen table. She put her arm around him.

Joff grinned at them. His gold teeth flashed.

'You got a lovely mum, son,' he said. He winked. 'You know that, don't you, lucky lad?'

Joe felt his mum's heavy breathing, the thudding of her heart.

'Go on, Joff,' she said. 'Go away now, please. Please. Don't come again.'

Joff just stood with his arms folded and a sweet smile on his face as he cast his eyes across her. Then he licked his lips.

'Put a word in for me, son,' he said, as he went away. ''Cos you got a lovely tasty mum.'

That night Joe's head was filled with Joff. Son, he kept on saying. Son. Joe dreamed of being a baby. He saw Joff inside the house with his arm around his mum. Joff leaned over him and grinned and simpered and reached down to tickle him. Joe woke gasping in the darkness. Was this a memory or just a dream? He went across the landing to his mum and climbed into bed beside her.

'Mum,' he whispered. 'Mum.'

She moved to make space for him and slept on.

'M-Mum.'

'Shhhhhhh.'

'Mum. Was J–Joff my d–da—'

She came slowly out of sleep.

'Your dad?'

'I dreamed . . .'

'Oh, Joe, it's just a dream. You know who your dad was. A daft bonny lad that spun the waltzer in the fair and your mother was a daft young lass. And you know I'm sorry about how you came but I'll never be sorry about you.'

'Not J—'

'Oh, Joe.' She sat up and stroked his hair and the moonlight shone in her eyes. 'Not Joff. Never Joff, no matter how many times he sniffs around.' She smiled. 'You and your dreams. Come on. Calm down.'

She sang a song from his early days.

'If I were a little bird, high up in the sky,
This is how I'd flap my wings and fly, fly, fly.
If I were a cat I'd sit by the fireplace . . .
This is how I'd use my paws to wash my face . . .

'You were the loveliest thing I ever saw, tiny bonny baby lying at my side. I knew from your very first cry that you'd feel things more than any other, be scared more than any other, be overjoyed more than any other.

I knew you wouldn't have an easy ride.' She smiled and shook her head and drew him closer. 'But your heart is filled with strength and goodness, Joe Maloney. You'll find your way.'

He lay against her. She sang again.

'If I were a rabbit small, in the woods I'd roam,
This is how I'd dig my burrow for my home.
If I were . . .

'It isn't easy, this life,' she breathed. 'But we have each other, Joe, and nothing can change that. Good night, love.'

'Good night.'

He went back to bed. He wanted to see himself driving Joff from the garden. But he felt so small, so young, so uncertain, and all that night and for many nights after he was filled with the image of Joff with his mum and the fear that Joff was his dad.

Five

'One day,' said Stanny, 'we're gonna stay out there for weeks. Real surviving. We'll live on what we can catch and kill. Back to nature. Mebbe we'll even do some raiding. Farms and things. Mebbe we'll end up going further and further out. Robbing and raiding and running from the law.'

Joe kept seeing the girl's face, the way she looked at him so easy from the doorway of the tent, the way she seemed so familiar, the way she seemed to know him, too. He recalled the tiger's sour scent, its vicious tongue, its teeth. It all seemed so familiar. Like a memory, not a dream. Joe turned and saw the summit of the tent against the sky.

'Used to be always like that,' said Stanny. 'Man against nature. Survival of the fittest. Kill or be killed. But today . . . You've never killed nothing, have you?'

'No.'

'You strike hard. You do it fast and clean. Joff'd show you. He likes you, you know.'

'L–likes?'

'Says there's something about you the other kids round here haven't got. Says he wants to help you to get tougher. He likes your mum and all. He says . . .'

Joe's head reeled. He didn't listen. He saw the teeth of the tiger sinking into Joff's throat, heard the tiger's growl of pleasure. He sighed.

'There was bears and wolves round here once,' said Stanny.

'Ages back.'

'Aye, ages back, but there's tales of panthers and things still living out there.' He lowered his voice, as if in secret. 'And we've heard them, Joe. Me and Joff. We've heard them things.'

'Heard?'

'We're lying in the heather in the dead of the night and we hear the breathing. "What's that?" I go. "Keep still," goes Joff. Dead dead still. Think me heart'll explode. The heather's rattling and trembling. There's something in the dark, something blacker than the night, something moving, creeping to us across the heather. There's something shining there, a pair of eyes. Joff's got his knife out and it's shining too. He hisses like a snake. He holds the knife up. "Be off!" he goes.

"Be off!" And it stops, it just stops dead still and watches us. Then it turns and we see it like the blackest shadow moving off again.'

'A panther?'

'I was little then. I said it was a devil. But we've talked about it since and said it must have been a panther, like they say is out there in those places.'

'Or a d-dream.'

'No dream. I saw its eyes. And its teeth. I know it would've killed me if Joff hadn't been there . . . You've got to come, Joe. If you come, you'll hear, and you'll mebbe even see.'

Joe narrowed his eyes, saw the winged creatures wheeling in the air. He imagined stepping through the Silver Forest, climbing through them to the Black Bone Crags. He felt the undergrowth beneath his feet, smelt the forest flowers. He lived in a dream, his mother said, and she was right. It was so hard to separate what existed in his head from what existed in the world. He blinked, shook his head, came back to Stanny Mole.

'We're going to kill it,' whispered Stanny.

'Eh?'

'Kill it. If we come across it again. We're going to cut its bloody head off and bring it home.'

Joe stared at him. He knew they would kill. Stanny already had skulls in his bedroom, boiled and bleached:

sheep skulls, rat skulls, badger skulls. They stood in a row on his windowsill.

'Why k-kill?' said Joe.

Stanny screwed his face up, like he was thinking.

'What kind of question's that?' he said. He thought again, then he laughed. 'How else'll we get the bloody head off it?'

His eyes shone, then he swivelled, with a knife clutched in his fist. There was a squealing from behind them, a high-pitched squeal of pain. But it was only a rabbit, attacked by a stoat. The rabbit was three times bigger than the stoat, but it lay there useless and jerked and squealed and let the killer do its work. Soon there was silence. Slick and bendy as a snake, the stoat ripped the flesh, lapped the blood and quivered in excitement. Maybe it caught the boys' scent. It turned its bloodied head and eyes and stared at them for a second, then darted off.

Stanny laughed.

'See? Nature in the raw, Joe. Cruel, cold.'

Joe knelt up, tried to see the stoat again.

'Back in its hole,' said Stanny. 'It'll be licking its fur, tasting the rabbit again, living the thrill again.' He thumbed the shining blade of his knife. 'That's what it's like out there. Back here, we're soft and getting softer. Just like Joff says.'

Six

They walked down past the Blood Pond to the ruins of Broomstick Farm. Stanny lit a fire on an ancient hearth in the Hag's Kitchen. He crawled through the weeds and the tussocky grass, cutting with his knife. He filled a bent aluminium pot with water from a slow stream and put the pot on the flames. He started to throw in what he'd found: clover, dandelion leaves, mushrooms. He cut thistle heads open and picked the nuts from inside, threw them in as well. The smoke swirled around them. The soup boiled and bubbled.

'Nature Stew,' said Stanny. 'The world's full of food for them that knows. Spring water, things that other folk think is just weeds.'

The fire died down, the soup went off the boil. Stanny wrapped his hands in his cuffs and lifted the pot on to a stone. He grinned and showed Joe four little speckled eggs.

'A speckled surprise,' he said. 'Skylarks' eggs. The final touch.'

He dropped them gently into the soup and they sank then slowly rose again and floated.

'Done to a turn. Go on, Joe.' He passed a twisted spoon to Joe. 'You're the guest. You go first.' Joe wrinkled his face. Stanny took the spoon back, dipped it in, drank, closed his eyes, chewed the bits. 'Absolutely delicious. Even if I say so myself.' He lifted an egg with his fingers and put it in his mouth, shell and all, and chewed and swallowed and smacked his lips.

'Yum-yum. This is what it's like, surviving. But imagine the stew with a wood pigeon in it, or the leg of a hare.'

He suddenly stabbed his knife into the earth and laughed.

'Die, pigeon!'

Joe took the spoon again, dipped it in, sipped. A weird sour taste. Silt on his tongue.

'Lovely, eh?' said Stanny. 'Go on, again, get some of the good bits this time, Joe.'

Joe sipped again. Bitter mushroom on the tip of his tongue. He swallowed. Stanny grinned, took the spoon and drank again. Then lifted an egg and held it to Joe's mouth.

'Go on,' he said. 'Shell and all. Yum-yum.'

He held it closer and Joe let him drop it between his

teeth. Held it a moment on the floor of his mouth, then bit. A taste like an egg, but saltier, sourer. The shell brittle and sharp. He licked it from the hollows of his mouth, from the cracks between his teeth.

'Wash it down,' Stanny said, and Joe sipped again. They each ate another egg. They spooned up the last of the soup. They sat against the broken wall and looked across the motorway towards the Black Bone Crags.

Soon Joe's body began to twitch. He rolled from side to side. The distant tiny skylarks yelled. He opened his eyes and the sky was filled with them. They darkened the sky from horizon to horizon, a storm of trembling black specks that sang in the vast blue space between the village and the sun. Above the crags, the peculiar winged beasts wheeled across the sky. He closed his eyes again, heard a single skylark singing at the centre of his brain, a sweet and frantic noise. Tasted its egg on his tongue, felt it trembling with life inside him. He stood up and crouched forward and gently stamped his feet on the earth. He turned slow circles. He let the skylark sing and fly. He gently stamped the earth. He groaned and let the noises in his throat become sweeter, sweeter, lighter, lighter. He spread his arms behind his back. He gently stamped his feet upon the earth. He sang. He trembled. He felt himself begin to disappear.

'Joe! Joe, man!'

Stanny rubbed his eyes, crouched low in the ruins, snorted. 'What you doing, Joe, man? You do the craziest things sometimes.'

Joe hesitated, mid-dance.

'What you doing?' said Stanny again.

Joe turned to him. What *was* he doing? He had no words for it, for the way his spirit sometimes soared inside him and blended with the earth and the sky. He had no words for the way his body trembled and seethed with such excitement.

'Just th-this,' he muttered. He closed his eyes, turned a circle, opened his eyes again. He looked upwards, to the pale blue tent, so beautiful. He started to walk up the slope towards it.

'And where you going?' said Stanny.

Joe peered back.

'Just th-there.' He pointed. 'Just to the tent, Stanny.'

Stanny clenched his fists.

'The tent! For what?'

Joe searched for words to explain how it drew him towards it.

'Sometimes you're hopeless,' said Stanny. 'It's time you bloody toughened up, Joe.'

Joe turned away, walked on.

'Five o'clock tomorrow morning,' Stanny said. 'Be there. Let Joff get working on you.'

Seven

Up he went beneath the larks and through the breeze. The roofs of Helmouth appeared. The great sloped circular wall of the tent filled more and more of the sky. The arm-thick guy-ropes creaked. On this side were the caravans and trailers of the circus people. Close to, he saw that they were ancient things. The frames were twisted, the tyres were treadless, the chrome was cracked.

An old man stared into the sky from a caravan window. His head rested on his hand. He broke into laughter as Joe passed by. He knocked on the window and pressed his face joyously against the glass.

'Tomasso!' he called. 'Tomasso! Tomasso! Oh, it's you! Isn't it? It's you!'

Joe hurried on. He shook his head violently.

'No,' he mouthed, 'No. M-my name is Joe!'

He chewed his lips in confusion.

'Tomasso!' called the man. 'Tomasso! Tomasso! Tomasso . . .' Until his lips were still and he looked to the sky again.

Half-naked children scampered here. A pair of little grey dogs in pink frocks trotted for a few seconds on their hind legs at Joe's side. He circled the tent, towards the billboards, a twisted ticket booth, the canvas door. A white-faced clown practised juggling, throwing up sticks and stones and rubbish he lifted from the ground. Then Joe saw her, the girl from the tent door. She sat on a little stool with some village kids around her and she painted their faces. Mothers stood and watched and smiled from nearby. The kids were animals. They were mice, cats, dogs, lions, tigers, bears. The girl painted with thin brushes. She held up mirrors so that each child could see his new face. The children raised their hands like claws and growled at each other. They padded on all fours across the wasteland. They raised their heads and sniffed the air. They leaped at imaginary prey. They killed. They licked their paws. They giggled and their mothers grinned. One of the children called Joe's real name. 'Joe! Joe! Look at me. Joe!' And the girl turned her eyes to Joe and smiled and held her paintbrush up and asked, 'So what will you be, Joe?'

He blushed and walked on and stood before the biggest billboard. The paint on it was flaking away. The sheets of timber underneath were cracked. The animals on it were clumsy and stiff, like they'd been painted by children. Lions, tigers, elephants, zebras roamed together through a forest of oak trees and sycamores, like an English wood, and there were daffodils growing and sparrows flying. In a clearing in the wood, people held hands and danced in rings. On a little hill was Hackenschmidt's Circus, a shining bright blue tent. The real blue tent was threadbare and faded and covered in patches. There was another billboard resting against the wall of the tent. It was an ancient blurry photograph of a barrel-chested man with his fists raised to show the muscles in his arms and the width of his chest.

GEORGE HACKENSCHMIDT
LION OF RUSSIA
WRESTLING CHAMPION OF THE WORLD
!! Throw him to THE EARTH and make YOUR FORTUNE !!

'The greatest wrestler the world has ever seen.'

Joe turned and there she was behind him.

'He was,' she said. 'George Hackenschmidt. The Russian Lion. Champion of the World. And he still performs every night. Can you believe it?'

'Yes.' He looked at the photograph. 'No.'

'No? You wouldn't say that to Hackenschmidt's face.'
She smiled. 'I saw you this morning, walking past with
your friend. Your name's Joe.'

'Yes.'

'And I'm Corinna,' she said. 'Corinna Finch. And this
is our owner, Hackenschmidt. So now we're all at
home.'

She watched him in silence. Her face was smooth
and pale and oval. Her skin was splashed with freckles.
Her eyes were brilliant sky-blue. She still wore the
grubby mac, fastened tightly at the waist, and black
tights and silver slippers.

'Would you like to look inside?' she asked.

Joe's eyes widened.

'C-can I?' he said.

She laughed, and turned to the heavy canvas door.
She held it aside.

'Come on,' she said. 'Nothing'll eat you, you know.'

Joe looked back at the painted children, the dancing
dogs, the village rooftops dark beneath the sunlight.
Then went to her, pushed his way into the tent and the
canvas slid smoothly over him. Corinna followed, and
let the door fall back into place.

Eight

Almost dead still. Almost dead quiet. Just the walls of the tent shifting gently in the breeze. Just the muffled drone of the city beyond the village that seemed a thousand miles away. So calm, in the subdued blue light. Joe breathed deeply. The scent of drying earth and grass, of old old canvas.

'Lovely, isn't it?' she said.

He nodded.

'Lovely.'

High up, in the summit of the tent, were the remnants of an ancient golden sun and silver moon and stars, faded to almost nothing. Below these were the trapeze, the high wires, the tiny platforms with the safety-net stretched below. A ladder dangled from the central pole.

They walked further in, stepped over a low wooden wall on to the sawdust and straw that lay in the ring. The sloping wooden benches circled them. The blue light fell on them and made them gently luminous.

'I work up there,' she said. 'Always have.' She tipped her head back and gazed upwards. 'But I'm not very good. None of us are. Hackenschmidt says it's because we've lost our way and our will and we're in our final days.' She turned her face to him. 'Did you hear us, in the night, when we came?'

'Yes.'

She watched him.

'Go on,' she said.

'I d–dreamed about you,' he said.

'What kind of dreams?'

He sighed. He smelt the breath, the pelt. He looked around himself, but there was nothing.

'Tell me,' she said.

'A tiger come,' he said.

She laughed suddenly, and turned away as if what he said was absurd, then she watched him again.

'We weren't sure why we came here,' she said. 'But maybe you're the reason, Joe.'

Joe blinked. He had no way of knowing what to say to this.

'I could swing for you,' Corinna said.

'Eh?'

'I could climb up for you and do some of my act for you.'

They looked up together towards the trapeze.

'Of course there's no one to catch me,' she said. 'Never is these days. I just do it all all alone, Joe. But I could swing, let go, and somersault down into the net. It would be something that you've seen. Well?'

'Dunno. Anything.'

'Dunno. Anything. You don't say much, do you?'

Joe shrugged, looked down.

'Words is . . .' he muttered.

'Words is?'

'H-hard,' said Joe. 'They get all t-tangled and tw—'

'Twisted?'

He raised his eyes and looked at her.

'Aye,' he said. 'Aye.'

She smiled.

'That doesn't matter,' she said. 'There's stronger things than words.'

Her eyes clouded. She toed the sawdust with her silver slippers. The tent flapped in the breeze and the huge central pole creaked and sighed.

'Once,' she said, 'when I started, when I was a little girl, I had a strong man as a catcher. Lobsang Page. Now he's in Las Vegas. Once, there were many many things.' She looked around the ring. 'Once, they used to run in with great sections of a cage. They put the sections all around the ring, so the whole ring was a cage.' She swept her arms out, showing the extent of it. 'Then they ran a low narrow cage to the outside of the tent. That's what the lions came through, and the tigers and the leopards. They growled and screamed and clawed the air and the ring was filled with wildness. The animals loved us, though. The trainers whispered into their ears and they did their acts for love.'

She watched Joe.

'You believe that?'

Joe blinked and saw the roaring beasts. He saw the trainers in shining clothes, dancing on tiptoe, holding whips and chairs.

'Yes.'

'Then my grandfather had his arm ripped off. Right here where we're standing.'

'W-what by?'

'A tiger. And mebbe that's when things started to change. When the animals stopped being close to us. When things would never be the same again.'

She looked up towards the trapeze.

'There's no t-tigers now?' Joe said.

She narrowed her eyes as she turned to him.

'What do you think, Joe?'

'I can't . . . tell.' He looked inside himself. He thought of last night. 'I think there are.'

She shook her head.

'No. There's no tigers now, Joe.'

She took off her coat. She wore a spangled costume. She quickly climbed the rope-ladder that dangled by the central pole. She climbed through the safety-net spread out above the ring. She stood on a tiny platform. She unfastened a trapeze and set it swinging back and forward beneath the faded stars and sun and moon. Then she leaped with her arms outstretched and held it tight. She swung from her arms, from her knees, moving gracefully through the blue shade, and her spangles shone and her face gleamed. Then she leaped, and tumbled, and seemed to hang motionless for a moment, held in the air above by nothing, as if she could stay there as long as she wanted. Then a somersault and she dropped into the net.

She lay there dead still then swung herself over the edge of the net and back to earth again.

Joe's eyes were shining.

'That was brilliant,' he said.

'No, it wasn't. My mother, now she was really something. And her mother . . .'

'Your m–mother? Where's she now?'

She toed the dust again.

'In Russia.'

'R–Russia?'

'She trains kids in circus skills.'

'She trained you?'

'She should have stayed longer and trained me for longer. She shouldn't have cleared off to bloody Russia.'

She put her coat back on.

'What else d'you want to see?' she said.

'D-dunno.' He stared at her, concentrated, tried to compose the question on his tongue. 'Where h-have I seen you before, Corinna?'

She shook her head.

'Nowhere.'

'When I saw you this morning . . . I was sure . . .'

She waited, patient, as he framed the words.

'Was sure,' he said, 'I'd s-seen you before.'

'I know that.'

'Have I?'

'Course not. I have never been to Helmouth and you have never been out of Helmouth.' She toed the sawdust and hung her head. 'But I thought it, too.' She watched him from the corners of her eyes. 'You don't know what it means, do you?'

'N—'

'When you recognise somebody you've never seen before, it sometimes means you were with them in another life.'

Joe breathed the dusty air. He looked down at his

hands, that shone with a blue light that seemed to come from inside them.

Corinna laughed.

'Maybe we were tigers together,' she said. 'Or elephants. Or a circus act way way back when it all started . . . Maybe we were each other's catcher, Joe. Maybe we were the greatest fliers the world had ever seen. Once, long long ago. You think it's nonsense.'

In his head, Joe leaped through empty air with his arms outstretched. He looked into Corinna's eyes, eyes he knew he'd seen before.

'No,' he said. 'Not n-non—'

'Whatever we think doesn't matter. If it's true, that we were together before, then it means there are things to do together in this life as well. And there'll be nothing we can do about it.'

She giggled as one of the grey dogs in frocks scuttled under the edge of the tent and tottered to them on its hind legs. She scooped the dog into her arms and smiled.

'Mebbe we were pretty little dancing dogs like you.'

Her face fell.

'I could be brilliant, you know,' she said. 'I could be as good as my mum.'

'I know.'

'She was so quick, so light. When she spun across the

tent they say she moved so fast she disappeared.' She looked at Joe again, as if daring him to disbelieve her. 'There were moments in her act, Joe, when she couldn't even be seen.'

Then she grinned, and turned the dog's face to Joe and it yapped and bared its teeth.

'This is Joe,' she said. 'He's nice. He looks little and weak and shy and words get tangled on his tongue but he's strong and brave, I think.'

The dog yapped again. Joe blushed again.

'I think we've come to the right place, little doggie,' said Corinna.

She moved towards the door. Joe followed. She held the flap back and bright daylight slanted across them.

'Who l-looks after you?' Joe asked.

'After me?'

'If your mum's gone?'

'The others here. Wilfred and Charley Caruso and Nanty Solo and . . . Good kind folk. And Hackenschmidt, of course.'

Joe looked out across the wasteland towards the Black Bone Crags. He wanted to point and tell Corinna to look. He wanted to ask her what she saw out there.

'Go on,' said Corinna. 'You'll soon be back. If you're who we think you are, you'll soon be back.'

Nine

The animal children still played outside. There were children giggling, dogs yapping, clowns dancing. A pot-bellied pig snuffled at the grass.

'Tomasso!' someone called, from miles away. 'Tomasso! Tomasso!'

Joe moved towards the village.

'Maloney!' someone barked. 'Joseph Maloney!'

Bleak Winters, Joe's Humanities teacher. A clutch of year-tens were at his back.

'Mr Maloney! How very nice to see you again.'

Joe just stood there, eyes downcast.

'After all this time!' he said. 'Thought our paths would never cross again!'

He strode towards Joe with his arm stretched out as if to shake his hand. Some of the kids followed, nudged each other, giggled, like lots of kids around him did. Others hung back, turned away, bored by his booming voice, his showing-off. Winters stretched out and took Joe's hand.

'Let me introduce our Mr Maloney,' he told them. 'And, Mr Maloney, let me introduce some of your fellow pupils from Hangar's High. Hangar's High. You may not remember it. A redbrick educational establishment. Your school, Mr Maloney. Yes, your school!' He turned to the others and lowered his voice. 'You may not yet have come across our Joseph Maloney, for he is an elusive little chap. Something of a star at the disappearing act.'

They carried computer-printed banners: **BAN THE CIRCUS; CIRCUS MEANS CRUELTY: LET THE ANIMALS GO; TAKE YOUR TENT SOMEWHERE ELSE.**

'Come and join us, Mr Maloney. This is our lesson for today, a bit of philosophy, history, political action. What right have we to use animals for our entertainment?'

He put his arm around Joe's shoulder.

'Come and join us, Joseph. If you are not with us then you are against us.' He snorted. 'Or are you already enlisted as the new tiger tamer?'

'There's no t-tigers,' said Joe.

Winters gasped. He raised a finger.

'Let us listen to the words of an expert! Let us listen to the words of one who has already been inside the charnel house.'

'There's no t-tigers!' Joe said. 'There's no w–wild animals! They're gone.'

He wriggled free of Winters.

'That's not the point, Joe,' said Francesca Placido, a skinny girl with a Tibetan hat on. 'What about the dogs? What about the pigs? It's not just tigers, it's the whole animal world we have to think of.'

'Well said, Francesca,' said Winters. 'Mr Maloney?'

Joe felt the lark singing inside himself and the tiger prowling inside himself. He looked at the teacher, and knew that Bleak Winters was never anything else except Bleak Winters. He looked at the children. He knew that they, like him, might have larks and tigers inside themselves, but they kept them hidden, and one day their larks and tigers might disappear, just like Bleak Winters' had. He wanted to tell them this, he wanted to draw them away from Winters and towards the tent and the wasteland but he didn't have the words.

He hunched his back, moved on.

'Get back to school!' Winters snapped. 'Get back to school or you'll be lost in your own stupidity.'

Joe listened to his larks.

'Tomasso! Tomasso! Tomasso!' called the old man's voice, fading to almost nothing.

Ten

Cody's lot were gone. Joe walked to the Cut. He crawled on the ground there: rubble, litter, dried-out mud, dog prints, cat prints, boot prints. He ran his fingers across the dried-out mud. No tiger prints. He sniffed the air. No tiger smell. Turned back again, circled the village, clambered over piles of heaped-up earth, over the ruins of old cottages, through the spaces where the swimming-pools were supposed to come, the supermarkets, the car parks. Circled the great tent, avoided Bleak and his hangers-on. Saw Stanny miles away moving through the ruins of Broomstick Farm, more smoke streaming across him. Imagined having been a tiger, having been a trapeze artist. Watched the Silver Forest and the Golden Hills and the Black Bone Crags as he walked. 'Tomasso, Tomasso,' came faintly through the air. Clambered through the ruins of old terraced houses. Came to the Blessed Chapel. Fragments of gravestones lay embedded in the earth around it. Fragments of words were written on what was left of the walls. Eroded by wind and rain, odd and ancient bits of prayers could still be deciphered:

God . . . Blessed art . . . thy kingdom . . . In Loving Memory of . . .

He knelt in the dirt and breathed the words passed down from children to children.

'Spirits of earth and air, listen to my words this day.'

He spat on his hands and wiped them slowly across the name of God.

'Protect my mum this day.'

He breathed deeply.

'Let her heart be refreshed and let her life be lightened and let all harm and evil be lifted from her.'

He took a five-pence coin from his pocket and dropped it through a narrow slot between the stones. It chinked into the space behind.

He closed his eyes, searching for another prayer.

'Protect the larks. Protect the tigers.'

He touched the name of God again.

'Our men,' he breathed. 'Our men, our men.'

He stayed there in the Blessed Chapel. Thick soft turf had grown on the ruined floor. He lay there, out of sight of Helmouth. He watched the sun sliding slowly through the sky, watched the summit of the blue tent shifting in the breeze. The gentle breeze flowed over him. He curled his knees up to his chest and slept, leaning on the blurred fragments of ancient prayers. In his dream he walked with Mum across the motorway and strode through the Silver Forest beneath a storm of larks. There were deer watching from the dappled shadows, owls from low branches, rabbits from dark entrances in the earth. She held his hand and they skipped towards the Black Bone Crags and their laughter echoed through the trees. Then his mum was replaced by another who walked lightly at his side. He was about to turn to her, to see her.

He woke. Kids from Hangar's High were nearby. A bunch of boys kicked a football and wrestled with each other. A couple of couples walked hand in hand. Dejected stragglers trailed rucksacks from their hands. Some cast their eyes across him then turned away. He saw faces of a few who had been almost friends an age ago. A group of kids from Joe's year, from his class, approached. He crouched in the chapel, kept his head down, focused his mind on making them go away.

'Alone, Maloney?'

A girl's voice, laughing, mocking. Boys' voices joined in.

'Alone, Maloney?'

He crouched there, didn't move, like the rabbit that the weasel took.

A rock bounced into the chapel, rolled to his ankle.

Another came, accompanied by much laughter.

'Let earth eat them,' he muttered to the earth. 'Let fire take them.'

'Only Maloney, lalalalaaaaa!'

Two boys prowled like tigers coming through grass to take their prey.

'Where was you today, Only Maloney?' they hissed.

'Swallow them, burn them, blow them all away,' he whispered.

He fingered the name of God. Nothing happened to them. They came closer, closer. He rolled his fists, clenched them.

'What you bloody doing?'

A new voice. It echoed across the ruins.

'What you bloody doing to him?'

The prowlers lifted their heads. They searched the landscape with their eyes. They stood, began to back away, back to their pack.

It was Joff, standing on a heap of stones.

They scuttled away from him, like crabs, like beetles. They kept turning their heads to him, muttering, but they moved away. He came to Joe, stood by the Blessed

Chapel. He swiped his hand across his face and watched. He shook his head.

'Boy,' he said.

Joe raised his eyes.

'Boy!'

'Y—'

'You got to harden up, boy.'

Joff stroked the snakeskin tattoo at his throat. He chewed his lips with his golden teeth. He beckoned Joe from the chapel.

'You think this is how you should be, boy?'

'N-no.'

'A father wouldn't've let you get like this,' he said.

Joe hung his head.

'Hiding in holes,' Joff said. 'Scared of your own shadow. He'd have done something about it.'

He reached down, took Joe's arm, drew him out.

'You need a man, boy. You know that?'

Joe saw the snake scales tattooed on the backs of his hands.

'And that mother needs a man, boy,' Joff said. 'You know that?'

'Y—'

Joe chewed his lips. Joff slid his hand around the back of Joe's neck and held him. He cupped Joe's chin in his palm.

'The lad says you want to come out with us. Surviving. That's true?'

'Y-yes,' he said. 'No,' he said inside.

'It'd be the making of you. You've seen the change I've wrought in Stanny Mole?'

'Y-yes.'

'Aye. I am not an easy master, boy. And I'll lead you into deepest danger. But lads that walk with me become survivors.'

He stroked Joe's cheek.

'I'll ring changes in you, boy.'

Joe watched Joff stride away, past the blue tent as if it wasn't there, out of sight across the slope. He picked earth, licked it.

'Spirits of the earth,' he breathed. He swiped his hand across the name of God. 'Give Joe Maloney the strength he needs today. Our men. Our men.'

He knelt there in the Blessed Chapel. He closed his eyes. The images of his life in Helmouth swirled within him. Then the image of the tiger came. It stared from the shadows, as if it waited for him.

Eleven

As he left, a rat moved through the Blessed Chapel, low to the earth, and took no notice of him. A skylark dropped on to a gravestone three yards away and held its crested head high for a second, then went up again. Hung high over him singing, then went further to a higher plane and hung there too to sing. Then higher and higher till there was nothing but its song, so sweet, so ardent, and so far far far away. He thought of Corinna's mother spinning through the blue light, spinning so fast she went out of sight. Where did she go during those moments?

He stepped across the stones.

He walked through Cody's lot to the Cut. They hardly noticed him. Their eyes were blinded by hate and they were yelling at the tent.

'Gyppo scum! Filth! Get back where you come from!'

They stamped their feet, thrust their chins forward, jabbed their fingers, shook their fists.

Beyond them, a couple of girls sat at the kerbside, holding dolls in the air as if they were flying.

'Look, Joe. Fairies!' They laughed.

He paused.

'See them fly!' they said.

He laughed with them.

'Yeah!' he said. He crouched and saw how ordinary dolls were transfigured by the children's vision. 'Yeah!'

He walked on. His mum would be back from the Booze Bin by now, her afternoon shift finished. He walked through the broken gate, along the path beside the house. He slipped in at the back door, into the kitchen. Cut himself a slab of bread, started to butter it.

'That's you, Joe?'

'Yeah.'

She came and stood in the doorway between the kitchen and the hall.

'The Wag Man came, Joe.'

'Yeah.'

'Yeah.'

They both hung their heads and sighed.

'Oh, Joe,' she said. 'What we going to do with you?'

He lifted his shoulders, sighed again.

'He said if you keep on wagging it they'll start proceedings.'

He glanced from the window to the pale blue tent, paler than the darkening sky.

'He said if they start proceedings it'll lead to fines for me.'

He chewed and stared.

'He said if they fine me and you keep on wagging it they could even end up taking you away.'

She watched him.

'Do you understand, Joe?'

He nodded.

'Is that what you want?'

'No, Mum.'

'Joe, you have got to go to school.'

'Yes, Mum.'

He stepped towards her and she held him close and whispered his name. It had gone on so long. Psychiatrists had pried into his brain. Social workers had pried into his home. Teachers had been gentle with him, stern with him, furious with him. The Wag Man had trailed him back and forth across the wasteland. Policemen had come calling. Nothing had tamed him. The choice was easy. The eerie wasteland or the gates and walls of school? In school, Joe didn't know the things he was supposed to know. He couldn't think the thoughts he was supposed to think. He chose the wilderness, the larks, the rats and rabbits and stoats. And he accepted the loneliness that went with this choice. He accepted the pangs of fear and shame.

His mum reached into a cupboard and took out a big jar of raspberry jam and put it on a bench.

'Spread some of that on it.'

He spun off the top, plunged in his knife, wiped it across the buttered bread.

She shook her head sadly.

'It's not easy. We need to make a new start somehow, Joe. But how do we do that? How do we change?'

'Dunno, Mum.'

'Some folk say you need a man at home, son. You think that?'

He caught his breath.

'Not . . . Joff!' he spat.

'No, love. Never Joff.'

She looked out into Helmouth while Joe dreamed of the tiger's jaws closing on Joff again.

'Mebbe we should move away,' she said, and laughed. 'There's a thought, eh? Get out of Helmouth. How many manage that?'

She licked her fingers and smoothed his hair.

'You,' she said. 'Like you been dragged through a hedge backwards. What you been doing out there, eh?'

'Walking. Looking at the circus. I made a f-friend.'

'A friend?'

'She's Corinna.'

'That's great, Joe. She's from the circus?'

'Yeah. She works on the trap—'

'The trapeze! Joe, that's great.' She laughed. 'I can see how the circus'd be your kind of thing. Tigers and—'

'There's no t-tigers.'

'No?'

'No. All gone.'

'But great all the same, eh?'

'Yeah.'

She held him at arm's length.

'You're such a funny'n, Mr Joseph Maloney. Always were, right from the start. Something different in your blood or something. But you know what I think?'

'No.'

'I think there's something very special about you. I think one day you'll amaze us all.'

She laughed.

'But mebbe that's nowt but a mother's love talking.'

Twelve

He sat in his room and watched the twilight come on. Soon she'd go out again for her evening shift in the awful Booze Bin. He smelt the food she was cooking for him. *A funny'n. Always been a funny'n.* She'd said that all through his short life. She used to say how beautiful he was when he was born. She used to say that on the night that he was born the sky was filled with shooting stars, like the universe was celebrating. She said the midwife told her he was the bonniest bairn she'd ever brought into the world. She said that his one green eye and his one brown eye were a sign of great good fortune. She said big brains and muscles didn't matter. It didn't matter that his dad was just some daft lad that spun the waltzer in a fair. What mattered was Joe's gentleness, his bravery, his great big joyous heart. What mattered was that she loved Joe and Joe loved her. And all through his life there had been hugs, and gentle words and laughter. But it was so hard for her. A young mother, a troubled son, little money, a home in Helmouth on the fringes of the world. He knew she needed him to grow and change and Joe didn't know how to do those things, and he hated hurting her, just hated hurting her. And hated those times the days ended as they sometimes did, when they cried together as evening fell on Helmouth and there seemed no way of getting back the light.

He licked the jam from around his lips and listened. There were people in the streets, walking to the tent. Footsteps, excited voices, the laughter and squeals of little ones. Soon he heard the trumpets and drums dinning the dusk. There was applause, laughter, gasps of excitement and joy. He imagined Corinna spinning so fast she disappeared. He heard a growl, like an animal's growl, but so deep it seemed to come from some dark deep cavern rather than from a creature's mouth. He lay still and listened. Nothing. He looked from the window. Nothing. Just an illusion. And anyway there were no tigers, there were no wild beasts, just dancing dogs and pot-bellied pigs.

He imagined Joff and Stanny preparing for tomorrow, packing their knives and hatches. He imagined their excited whispers: how far they would go, what they would take, what they would kill. He imagined them talking about himself, talking about what they would do to make him a man. He imagined Joff licking his lips as he talked about the lovely tasty mother. He shuddered.

'Joe!' she called from downstairs. 'Joe! Dinner's done.'

He went down to her, sat at the kitchen table. They ate sausages and potatoes and peas and grinned and sighed at how delicious they were.

'A f-feast!' said Joe.

'Truly a blooming feast!'

He poured a shining pool of ketchup on to his plate and dipped bread into it.

'Fit for a . . . king!' he said.

'And a queen!'

Soon she looked at the clock and hung her head like a stupid thing and groaned the words,

'Booze Bin, Booze Bin, come on, boozers, get your drink. Still, if they didn't need their drink, there'd be no job for me. You'll stay in tonight, Joe?'

He shrugged, chewed the sausage.

'Might go for a w—'

She raised her eyes.

'Not too far, love.'

'No,' he said.

'Good lad.'

She stroked his brow. She used to forbid these walks.

But she knew his passion for the night, and as he grew older she began to give way. What was it about darkness? Was it the cover it gave, protecting him from those who mocked by day? Or was it the night's intensity, the way that the moon and the stars and the blackened world vivified his dreams?

She kissed him. She knew he wouldn't stray far. He would return to her intact.

'Take care,' she whispered.

He watched her leave the house, pass beneath the streetlights, disappear into Helmouth's gathering night.

Thirteen

He followed, a few minutes later. He went into the wasteland. No Cody's lot. The great tent glowed beneath the stars. Silence outside, applause and laughter inside. Not a soul to be seen. Joe circled the tent, went to the back of it. In the caravans, a few lights burned behind curtains. Low down, headlights traced the motorway. The Black Bone Crags bulged high against the night. Joe dropped to his knees and crawled on all fours beneath the arm-thick guy-ropes. He heard the canvas flap and creak and rustle. He burrowed, like an earthbound creature, shoving his head between the tent and the grass, pulling the great weight of blue material across himself, slithering through.

Above him was a bank of benches, bottoms and dangling legs. He peered through the boards and legs. The dogs were dancing in the ring. Their master was a dainty man with a goatee beard who teetered on tiptoe.

He conducted the dogs with a pointed white stick. He kept turning, bowing to the scattered spectators. A few of them applauded. There was mocking laughter. There were cries of scorn. The dogs kept tumbling, falling across each other. Sometimes they lost concentration and wandered round the ring alone with their noses to the dust as if they searched for something. In the end, the master gathered them all into his arms and gave a final bow. Sweet wrappers and lollipop sticks were thrown into the ring. The crowd mocked and groaned. The master whispered to his dogs as he carried them out. He stroked and petted them. Joe imagined his whispered words, like the words his mother used to use for him: 'It's all right, my sweets. Take no notice of them, my sweets. They're jealous, that's all. You are bright and beautiful and brave.'

Clowns tumbled across the ring. Corinna came. She wore the tightly fastened raincoat. She carried a tray of ice creams at her waist. She took money, gave out ice creams, nodded and smiled as music crackled around her head. Holes in her tights, holes in her shoes. Joe stared, stared hard, willed her to look through the bodies, to look through the crowd and the benches, to see him there, his hungry eyes shining in the dark. But she didn't look, she didn't see him there. Behind her, two men in black entered the ring. They carried chains and nets across their shoulders. They hauled on a rope and Hackenschmidt's cage lurched into the ring

Rusty iron bars, rusty iron padlock. Hackenschmidt wore a filthy white vest, filthy white leggings covered in dark and bloody stains. He had great arm and leg muscles, a huge round belly, a long black filthy beard, drooling red mouth, matted hair, glaring eyes. He grunted and groaned and glared. He reached out through the bars and clutched the air. There were gasps, giggles, muttered curses. Mothers and fathers gripped each other's hands and put their arms around their children. Girls screamed in horror and delight. Lads stood and snorted and beat their chests. And then the drumbeat stopped and a man all dressed in shining red came in. He carried a gun in one hand, a megaphone in the other. The crowd grew quiet. He put the mega-phone to his lips.

'Here is Hackenschmidt,' he said. 'Here is the Lion of Russia, the greatest wrestler the world has ever seen. This is the true Hackenschmidt,' said the man in red, 'who was here long before any of us were born, and who will be here long after each of us has died. He has come to challenge you. Do not be frightened. There is tenderness deep inside his heart. He has beaten nobody as far as death. And we will protect you.'

Hackenschmidt stood silent. He held his head to one

side, as if listening to something far away. The man in red turned to the guards who had dragged the cage in. He raised the gun towards the cage.

'Bring him out,' he called, and the guards stepped forward, unlocked the padlock, and stood back.

Hackenschmidt lumbered out. He thumped his fists against his chest. He circled the ring. In the front rows, the people cringed. They tried to shuffle back to the upper rows. A mother and her children fled through the heavy canvas doors.

'Knock him down and win a thousand pounds!' said the man in red. 'Who'll be the first to accept his challenge?'

Hackenschmidt drooled and glared. Arms as thick as legs, legs as thick as trees, head big as a bull's. The great belly, the bloodstains. And even in his secret place, Joe caught the stench of him, the sweaty bloody animal aroma of him.

'AAARRRRGGGGGHHHHHHHH!' groaned Hackenschmidt. 'EEEEUUUUUURRRRRRRR-RRRRRRGGGGGGG!'

He lurched at the crowd and the guards beat him back with their chains. The crowd yelled in fear and horror and joy. A lad jumped into the ring and quickly jumped back out again.

'Come on,' said the man in red. 'Come in pairs, come

in threes. Take on Hackenschmidt and win a thousand pounds! You, sir? How about you, sir? Or even you, madam? Or you, young miss?'

A bald-headed man stepped into the ring, Nat Smart, a man from the village, a man Joe had often seen jogging through the streets. He circled Hackenschmidt then rushed at him with his fists. Hackenschmidt flipped him to the earth, he was dragged away. Two lads from school approached from opposite sides and grabbed an arm each. Hackenschmidt squeezed them against his belly then flung them away. Others came, running, prowling. They tried to knock him down with force, or to trick him with trips. They leaped on to his back, they crawled between his legs. Hackenschmidt swatted them like flies or held them tight and squeezed the breath from them before shoving them away. He lurched and groaned and thumped his chest. Soon no one went to him. Then he turned his face to Joe. He stared through the legs, through the benches, to the two eyes that shone out of the dark hiding place. Joe stared back at the filthy face, the red-rimmed glaring eyes. Hackenschmidt was dead still, then he stepped forward, mouth hanging slack, teeth bared, great filthy hands reaching out for Joe. Joe moved backwards as the guards caught Hackenschmidt. They shoved a bloody bone into his fist and he chewed it. He staggered backwards,

63

chains around his neck, gun barrel at his temple. He entered the cage again. The cage was locked and dragged out again, taken out of the tent again.

Clowns tumbled across the ring. Corinna came. She took money and gave out ice creams. Joe crouched deep in the dark, against the canvas. She didn't look at him. He burrowed out again, into the night again.

Fourteen

He moved through the wasteland, to where he could no longer see the lights of Helmouth, just the orange glow that hung in the air above it. The moon shone over the distant Black Bone Crags. Headlights streaked the motorway. The blue tent glowed. Joe crouched on the earth, allowed the night to enter him. He thought of the snakeskin on Joff, the skylark speckles on Corinna, the animal roars of Hackenschmidt. He knew how the lives of people and the lives of beasts could merge out here in the wasteland. He knew what it was to be Joe Maloney but also more than Joe Maloney. Out here by day he could rise into the blue like a skylark. At night he could flicker through the darkness like a bat. He emptied his mind now of being just Joe Maloney. He felt weasel fur growing on the backs of his hands. He felt claws where his fingers were. He hissed and he was a snake slipping through ancient cellars beneath the Blessed Chapel. He crouched on all fours and his face and teeth sharpened as he took on the shape of a fox. Nobody knew that he knew how to do these things. They were secret, things that grew from his secret heart.

When he was a small child, he saw more than other small children did. He used to point to the air above the Black Bone Crags and try to name the things he saw, but no one else ever saw them. There were moments when his mother seemed about to see, when she raised her eyes and followed his finger to where he pointed and her eyes widened and she whispered, 'Yes, Joe. I think . . . there's something . . .' And she used to listen when he raised his finger and told her to listen to the weird songs and whispers he heard on the air. And she used to smile and encourage the drawings he made when he was small, of the beasts and fairies he saw and played with in the long weeds and grasses of their garden. She never scoffed, she never scorned, but he knew she never truly heard and never truly saw and never truly understood. He knew that no one ever truly understood.

One day, in the first days of his truanting, days when those who grew with him in Helmouth had begun to turn away from him with their strange mixture of spite and fear, Joe wandered weeping in the wasteland. He found a boy crawling in the Hag's Kitchen, scratching at the earth and whining. He crouched and watched and listened. The boy dug at the earth with his fingers, tearing away little bits of turf, dragging out little heaps of soil. He puckered his mouth and nose and sniffed and snorted like a little beast. Then he turned and saw Joe there and he flinched and held up his hands like paws in protection. The two boys watched each other and the boy in the Hag's Kitchen returned to being just a boy again. Joe said nothing, didn't know how to say anything.

'I was being a mole,' said the boy. 'My name's Stanny Mole so I was being a mole.' He tipped his head to one side, daring Joe to challenge him. 'OK?'

'O-OK,' said Joe. Then he pointed to the air above the Black Bone Crags. 'They f-fly,' he stammered.

And Stanny looked and his eyes widened for a moment and Joe thought that Stanny Mole was on the brink of seeing, but then Stanny lowered his eyes again to the earth and said,

'What fly?'

Stanny Mole was a newcomer to Helmouth, sent from the city to live here with his mother. He was a boy already used to truanting, a boy who was more hardened to loneliness than Joe, a boy who right from the start told Joe that he needed to toughen up. But he

67

became Joe's friend and they spent many days together wandering the wasteland. Then Joff entered Stanny's life and began to take him across the motorway into the Silver Forest and up towards the Black Bone Crags and he began to teach Stanny how to survive and kill out there. And they wanted Joe to go with them, out into those places of wildness and vision and dream, but Joe held back. He knew if he ever did go there, it must be with someone who saw what he saw and felt what he felt, someone who was a true partner, a true friend. Someone who understood what it meant to move from Helmouth towards the furthest fringes of the world, towards the furthest fringes of the mind.

Joe sniffed and shivered. His ears were alert to the night. He trembled, heart fluttered, muscles twitched. What had he almost heard, what had he almost seen roaming the wasteland further downhill, further away from the light? He crouched and watched. Nothing. Behind him, the crowd in the tent clapped and jeered. He imagined Hackenschmidt lapping blood from meat in his locked cage. He imagined Corinna spinning, spinning, spinning. He imagined Stanny dreaming of the panther. He imagined his mum in the Booze Bin, selling cigarettes and cheap lager to Cody's lot.

'Spirits of the air and earth,' he breathed, 'protect us all tonight.'

He twitched again. What roamed the wasteland, further out into the dark? He peered. Nothing.

'Spirits of water and fire, spirits of the moon, spirits of the stars, protect us all. Our men. Our men.'

He crawled on hands and knees away from it, towards Helmouth's lights, into the great pool of blueness cast by the tent. A shadow moved across the wall of the tent, high up. A flying swinging thing. Corinna. He thought of her eyes, her speckled skin. He dreamed another shadow moving there, back and forth across the first, the shadow of another flier, a catcher from another time, another life. The scattered crowd applauded. There came a growl, like the growl of an animal echoing from a deep dark cave. He turned, cast his eyes across the wasteland. Nothing. But he began to move quickly back to Helmouth.

Fifteen

Joe was exhausted by his day. Went straight to bed, lay there drifting in and out of sleep, disturbed by the folk returning from the tent, their feet on the pavements, their laughter. He wouldn't sleep properly anyway till he'd heard her key in the lock. Pale orange light filtered through his curtains from the streetlights. Joe gazed at his curtains, at the little mirror on his wall, at his half-open door, at the old pictures still stuck with Sellotape to his wall, at the heap of his clothes on the floor. These things shifted and merged and changed. Nothing was fixed. Nothing was simply itself. The patterns of light and dark brought weird beasts to life, built weird cities, weird landscapes. Joe watched, and tried not to be afraid, and sometimes slept, and then jumped back from weird dreams to this weird form of waking. He sighed. He chewed his lips. If he grew, if he toughened up, would all this shifting stop?

She turned her key in the lock.

She called upstairs.

'Joe! You're in?'

'Yes, Mum!'

She came up to him, sat on his bed, her eyes reflecting the pale orange light.

'How's my boy?'

'F–fine.'

'You had a walk?'

'Yes. Not too far.'

She stroked his brow.

'When you've grown up,' she said, 'we will go far. We'll get out of Helmouth. We'll move, just like those people in the circus move. We'll find a lovely life, Joe, you and me.'

He heard her gently beating heart, her gentle breath.

'L–love you,' he breathed.

'Yes,' she said. 'Love you.'

And started to sing, sending him to sleep.

'If I were a little bird, high up in the sky.
This is how I'd flap my wings and fly, fly, fly.
If I were a cat I'd sit by the fireplace,
This is how I'd use my paws to wash my face.
If I were a rabbit small, in the woods I'd roam,
This is how I'd dig my burrow for my home.
If I were . . .

'Good night,' she whispered. 'Good night, little one.'

She went downstairs. Soon she came up again to her own bed, her own sleep.

Joe slept. The night deepened. The tiger began to move again, out of the wasteland towards Joe Maloney.

Joe smelt it, the hot, sour breath, the stench of its pelt. He felt the animal wildness on his tongue, in his nostrils. He heard the beast padding up the stairs. He heard the long, slow breath, the distant sighing in its lungs, the rattle in its throat. It came into his room, it stood over his bed.

'Tiger,' he gasped. 'Tiger. Tiger.'

He prepared to die as the great striped face came closer, as the great curved fangs opened, as the cruel cold eyes stared into him. And then he changed. He felt fur beginning to break through his skin. He felt heavy paws and lethal claws. He felt his breathing deepen. He felt a tiger heart drumming in his chest. He rolled on his bed. Through his head rushed memories of running through hot grassland, antelope leaping before him, tigers alongside him.

'Tiger! Tiger! Tiger!'

It came from the night.

'Tiger! Tiger! Tiger!'

And the tiger took its wildness and its scent away, and Joe became simply Joe again and he went to the window and made a funnel of his hands and peered out and saw the orange stripes beneath the orange lights and the black stripes against the black night as the tiger loped towards the huge dark figure waiting there in the Cut.

'Tiger!' Joe whispered, and the tiger turned, and looked at the boy in recognition. Then was gone, disappearing with the man beyond the Cut.

Joe Maloney stroked his hands, licked his teeth, listened to his heart.

To the east, beyond the village, above the Black Bone Crags, a thin line of orange striped the black sky. Joe Maloney dressed himself, tiptoed from the house, followed the tiger, and the scent of tiger was on him, and the memory of tiger was running through his blood.

SATURDAY

One

Easy breath, easy heart. The scent of sawdust, canvas, animal skin and animal dung. Soft earth beneath him. Gentle noises: creaking and flapping of canvas. He lay there. Something moved across his face. Something soft, delicate that stroked his skin.

'Joe. Joe. Joe Maloney.'

He opened his eyes.

Corinna knelt at his side with a thin paintbrush in her hand. Beyond her was the net, the trapeze, the faded galaxy. Over everything, the blue blue light.

'I knew you were here, Joe,' she whispered. 'I dreamed that you were here. I knew you'd come. And here you were, fast asleep.'

She showed him the paintbrush, her little case of paints.

'Turning you into a tiger,' she said. 'A disguise. Hold still. Nearly done.'

He lifted his fingers to his face but she stopped him.

'You'll smudge it, Joe.'

'A tiger came for me,' he said.

She smiled.

'A tiger?'

She continued to paint him, orange, black and white. Then passed a glass of warm milk to him. He sat up and sipped and licked his lips.

'Straight from one of our goats,' she said. 'There are no tigers, Joe.'

She gave him toast, saturated with butter.

'Eat this.'

He sat up and ate the food and drank the milk. Her skin was so smooth, so speckled, just like a skylark's egg-shell. Her eyes the deepest blue. She wore the tightly fastened mac over her spangled costume, black tights, spangled slippers. He peered at the trapeze. He imagined jumping, spinning so fast that he disappeared. She handed him some neatly folded clothes, black satin shirt and trousers.

'Put these on,' she said. She sniggered, turned round. 'Go on, then.'

He quickly took off his jeans and T-shirt, and put the new things on. She giggled when she turned round.

'Those boots, Joe! We'll have to see about those as well!'

He stood there awkward, blushing beneath his tiger stripes. He looked up again. In his head he leaped through empty air.

'I'd l-like to go on that,' he said. 'That rope. I want to d—'

She grinned.

'Oh, Joe. You'll have me strung up.'

'I'd like—'

'It's against the rules. It's against the law. You'll get me sacked and us shut down.'

'N-nobody'd know.'

'You break your back and nobody'd need to know.'

He looked down, thought of falling from thin space on to the solid earth, thought of his back cracked in two, thought of lolling stupidly in his bed for a lifetime.

Corinna giggled.

'It's OK,' she said. 'Just joking. Course you can have a go. But not in those boots. And anyway, first we go to Nanty Solo.'

'Nanty S—?'

'She told me to take you to her if you came. Don't worry. She won't eat you up.'

79

Two

She led him from the tent. The paint on his face made the skin tight, inflexible. His dark satin clothes flowed and flapped, allowed the air through, so cool. Helmouth's windows glared in the early morning light. He looked across towards the motorway, but Stanny and Joff would already be far gone, probably already climbing through the Silver Forest.

Someone called, 'Tomasso! Tomasso! Tomasso!'

The man with the goatee beard stumbled out of a caravan. He wore a grubby white dressing-gown. He threw scraps of bacon to his little dogs. He smiled and waved at Corinna.

'Lovely Wilfred,' she said. 'He'll not go away from us.'

They moved towards the back of the tent. Caravans and trucks were coated with dust. Many tyres were already flat, and the vehicles slumped into the long grass, like they'd never move again.

'Tomasso! Tomasso! Tomasso!'

'That's Charley Caruso,' said Corinna. 'Greatest knife-thrower the world had seen. Then his son died in the Ring of Fire. Tomasso. He was only five years old.'

'He called me T-Tomasso.'

'He thinks that every boy might be Tomasso. And maybe one time he'll be right. Maybe his Tomasso will come back to him one day.'

'But if he's . . .'

'They threw him through the blazing ring. It had always been dead safe. He'd done it every night since he was three. But that night the spinning fire caught an edge of his clothes. It burned so quick. Burns and shock, and he was such a tiny thing.'

'Tomasso! Tomasso!'

'They wanted to take him away from us. But he wanted to stay, wanted to keep on travelling with us. Said it was the only way he'd see so many boys, the only way he might find his lost Tomasso again. Now he stares at the audience every night, stares into the face of every boy. He's another that'll never leave.'

They wandered on across the stony earth.

'Maybe you *are* Tomasso,' said Corinna. 'Maybe you are and you don't know it. Maybe we're all something else and we don't know it.'

'Mebbe,' muttered Joe.

'What do *you* think you might be?' she said.

Joe screwed up his face. He knew that others saw a small scared thing. He knew that he was a quiet awkward thing. But he knew that this awkward thing called Joe Maloney could be many things: a lark, a fox, a bat, a snake. He watched Corinna. He wanted to tell her what he knew and dreamed about himself. But the words stumbled on his tongue. He shuffled and shrugged.

She smiled and reached out and touched the stripes on his cheeks.

'Joe Maloney the tiger,' she said. 'Here we are.'

Three

A tiny timber caravan, blue like the tent, the paint flaking and cracking. There were remnants of old words above the door: Fortune, Future, Stars. Corinna knocked, then took Joe's hand, stepped inside, closed the door again. Pale light from the single small window. Tiny gas-lights flickering on the walls. The smells of candles, gas, urine, cats. A narrow low-roofed place. Threadbare red carpets covering the floor and walls.

'Corinna.' A low cracked whisper. 'You brought him, my Corinna.'

Small and scrawny, she sat in a narrow bed. Red hair with silver roots, a threadbare cardigan across her shoulders. Her cheeks were shrunken, almost corpse-like, but her eyes gleamed in the shadows as she turned her face and smiled upon Corinna.

On the walls, illuminated by the gas-light, were photographs of ancient scenes. Ancient caravans with ponies resting alongside them. Great tents with animal cages outside. Photographs of inside: bears and elephants, tigers snarling, lions roaring, horses leaping, panthers prowling, zebras, buffalo, llama, leopards, all of them within great tents, all of them watched by thousands of goggling eyes. Trapeze artists flew and somersaulted through the empty air. Men balanced great rocks and balls of steel above their heads. They supported pyramids of other men.

'I smell him,' said Nanty. 'Bring him nearer.'

'His name is Joe Maloney,' replied Corinna.

'A timid deer kind of thing. Let us touch him.'

Joe recoiled, but Corinna only smiled and took his hand and held it to the woman, who touched it with her twisted fingertips like claws.

'Her name is Nanty Solo,' said Corinna. 'Say, "Hello, Nanty Solo." '

'H–hel—'

'He has trouble with words,' said Corinna.

'Words?' said Nanty. 'That's no matter. Words is babble and noise and nonsense, Joe Maloney. But you know that, don't you?'

Joe chewed his lips. There was a pale membrane stretched across her eyes, clouding her iris and pupil, but it was as if she saw through this thing and right into his heart. She squeezed his hand and grinned.

'What is words beside a lark song, eh?'

Above her eyes, just above her eyebrows, there was a scar, a horizontal band of red that stretched straight across into the darkness beneath the thin red hair. A line as if at one time her head had been sawn or slashed in two, as if the top third had been lifted off and placed back down again.

'Your flesh is soft as buttercups,' she said. 'And I see enough to see that my Corinna's been at you, boy. What is it? Ah, tiger. Bless you both. Where you come from?'

'H-Hel—'

'They let you out of there?'

She wheezed and cackled and doubled up on herself. Corinna smiled.

'Nanty is lovely,' she whispered. 'She'll do you no harm.'

The ancient woman and the young girl contemplated the tiger-faced boy. Joe took his hand from Nanty, turned away towards a group of pictures. There was a blurry Polaroid, white animals grazing in the circus ring. Joe leaned close: squat little things, their horns growing in twists and curves. He leaned closer. He moved his head aside so that whatever morning light there was could fall upon the picture. And what he thought was true: each animal had just one horn growing at the centre of its head.

Nanty cackled.

'Unicorns. Yes. You ever see their like before?'

Joe shook his head and stared again. Beside the unicorns was a much older picture: a huge sleeping tiger in a net, carried by bearers on long poles from the edge of a dense forest. Then another: a tiger again, in a net again being carried by bearers through the open flap of Hackenschmidt's Circus. He tried to match the tiger that entered the tent with the tiger that left the forest.

Nanty laughed.

'Come back to Nanty, Joe. Let her smell you true. Let her divine you.' She tipped her awful head to one side. 'You been this way before?'

'N-n—'

'He lives here,' said Corinna.

'Ah! An' don't we all. No memory of being any other place? No memory of travelling with a bunch like us?'

'N-no,' said Joe.

Nanty drew Joe towards her. She bent down and sniffed his throat. She ran her fingers through his hair and sniffed her hands. She held her open hands below Joe's face.

'Spit in here,' she said.

Corinna nodded: Just do it, Joe.

86

He licked his dry mouth and spat, a sparse spray that glistened in tiny droplets on the dark creased skin of her palms. Nanty giggled.

'That's all? But it'll do.'

She raised her hands to her nostrils and breathed in deeply.

She caught Joe's hand and lifted it to her mouth. She licked his palm.

'Nice,' she whispered. 'Nice, nice.'

'Yes,' said Corinna.

Nanty's pale eyes softened as she pondered.

'And who'd you say your father and mother was?'

'I–I—'

Corinna clicked her tongue.

'Just tell her, Joe.'

'Mum's in Helmouth. Works in B–Booze Bin. Dad spun the w–waltzer in a fair.'

'One of that crew. And he's gone and left you long time back.'

'Y–y—'

'Step closer. Let Nanty listen to your heart.'

She took his elbow and rested her ear against his chest. Joe felt his heart quickening, thumping.

'Aye,' she whispered. 'The heart is beating in you as it should, then far beyond it is the secret one, like some creature panting in a deep dark cave.'

She reached beneath the covers on her bed, drew out a broad shallow wooden box. On the lid of the box was a tracery of silver. Nanty lifted the lid. In the pale light, Joe saw teeth, feathers, claws, fragments of bone, fragments of fur. Nanty closed the lid and gently rattled the box. She tipped her face closer to Joe.

'Corinna's right in picking you out, boy. Nanty gets the taste of something old and animal in you. You're not at rest in that world out there, is you, Joe Maloney?'

'N-n—'

'That's why words is such a trouble to you, boy.' She turned her eyes towards her window, towards Helmouth. 'The things you know is mebbe not suitable for the words and the world that exist out there.'

She rattled the box again.

'But look at these things, Joe. Look at the world that's in this box. These,' she hissed, 'is relics. Precious precious things. Bits of a world that was here before and that's here still for them that knows how to see.'

Joe reached towards the box but she held his hand, held him back.

'Not yet,' she crackled. 'Look into my eyes. Forget Nanty Solo's scar. Forget the world out there. Just look into the milky eyes of Nanty.'

He looked into her eyes, but still he saw the deep channel cut horizontally across her skull, still he saw the deep fault-line, still he wondered what kind of weapon and attack could have done this.

'Now close your eyes, boy.'

Joe closed his eyes. He felt Nanty's hands cradling his head, and he felt how tender they were.

'How can a thing like a head be held within a lady's fingers?' she whispered. 'Here's dreams and memories and ancient tales that's being told and told. Here's stars that shine a billion miles away and deep dark caves and forests and Helmouth and teachers and mothers and horns of unicorns and the stripes of tigers. Here's a thing that's bigger than the world and all the worlds there ever was. And look. All held within a little tent of tender bone and skin and cradled in a lady's fingers. How can this be so?'

Joe licked his lips, attempted no answer.

'There's them that say they know how it is so. They look inside the tender bone and skin and tell us what's inside and how it came to be there and what's right in there and what's wrong in there.' She sighed. Her fingers shifted, and it was as if they melted, and began to mingle with the bone and skin of his skull. 'There is them that has already tried to tell you this, Joe Maloney. Isn't there?'

'Y-y—'

'Do not believe them when they tell you, Joe Maloney.'

He heard the squeak of the lid as she opened the box.

'What would happen if Joe Maloney's head was lifted open? What would happen if they looked inside to take something out? What would happen to Joe Maloney's worlds?'

'Dun–dunn—'

'Nor does Nanty. Where does the dreams go when the tent of bone is broke?'

She opened the lid of the box. Joe heard skylarks screeching, rabbits squealing, cats yowling. The tiger prowled. Beasts flapped across the Black Bone Crags and padded through the Silver Forest.

'Touch,' said Nanty Solo. 'Take something out.'

Joe's fingers scrabbled in the shallow box with his fingertips, felt the sharp edges of bone and teeth, the lightness of feathers, the density of fur. His fingers closed on something hard, sharp, brittle.

'Bone,' breathed Nanty. 'Bless you.'

Joe looked. A greying fragment rested on his palm.

'Bone,' she said again. She licked it, pondered. 'Bone of a tiger if I'm not mistaken. Back in the twenties, or mebbes further back. Well chosen, boy.'

She snapped off a tiny fragment with her thumbnail.

'Swallow it,' she said.

Corinna nodded: Swallow it, go on.

'Will match up with the tiger in yourself I tasted,'

said Nanty. 'Will prepare you for the coming torments. Let me see your tongue.'

Joe opened his mouth, rested his tongue on his lower lip. She pressed the bone fragment on to the tip of his tongue.

'Swallow the bone of the tiger,' she said.

Joe swallowed, felt the tiger bone slipping past his throat and entering his darkness.

'You must say, "I thank you",' said Nanty.

'Th-th—'

'Say it.'

'I . . . th-thank you.'

Nanty Solo closed the box.

'Amen,' she whispered. 'Amen.'

She smiled.

'Make me tea, Corinna.'

Four

They sat on Nanty Solo's bed, sipped tea from little silver cups and nibbled ginger biscuits. Outside the dusty window, the day began in Helmouth. People moved in and out of the estate. Kids dawdled by the entrance to the Cut. The distant motorway dinned. Joe turned his face from the window. He pressed his cheek out with his tongue and felt the taut striped covering of paint there. He moved his shoulders beneath the cool dark clothes. He glanced at the unicorns and the tigers. He looked upon his friend Corinna who could fly and his friend Nanty Solo who had fed him ancient tiger bone. He leaned back against the wall, here in the ancient gas-lit caravan beside the great blue fraying tent. He breathed gently and listened to the gentle running of his blood, and he felt at home.

'In the beginning,' whispered Nanty Solo, 'everything was new. The tent, the tent poles, the ropes, the pegs, the caravans. Long long time back. The writing of the names was bold and bright. The moon and sun and stars was bright as silver and true gold. Beasts was carried from the darkest and the furthest corners of the world, and they prowled in gleaming cages and in the darkest and furthest corners of the brain. Men had learned to be strong as lions. Girls had learned to fly like birds. On the first of all nights, the tent was raised in a green field outside a great city. At dusk the stars came out in an inky sky and shone upon it all. The city glittered like a sky upon the earth. Between the earth and sky the blue tent glowed. And people left the city and walked out into the green field and into the glowing tent and they looked in astonishment at all that occurred before them in the sawdust ring. Tigers roared, girls flew, men as strong as lions lifted many men. Soon the tent moved on, to other cities, other fields. But it also stayed, and glowed for ever after in the dreams of those who had entered it.'

She sipped her tea and sighed.

'Now we are mocked and spat upon. We scurry from wasteland to wasteland. We are part of no one's dreams.'

She smiled at Joe.

'No one's except those like you, I think, Joe Maloney.'

'Y-yes,' said Joe.

'The tiger come for you last night,' she said.

He gasped. 'Y-y—'

'It come to find you.'

'Y-y—'

'It come for you for you will be the one to take the tiger out.'

Joe stared at Nanty, at Corinna. They smiled back at him.

'Wh-what?' said Joe.

'It's OK,' said Corinna. 'There are no tigers, Joe.'

'That's right,' said Nanty. 'There is no real tigers.'

She pressed a twisted finger to his lips.

'One day not too far away, there'll be bits of me and Hackenschmidt and Charley Caruso and good Wilfred rattling round inside this relic box.'

She put the box back beneath the covers.

'And further off, mebbe bits of my Corinna and bits of you, my Joe Maloney.'

She gazed out through the tiny window, towards the folk resting, playing, passing by, towards the tussocky grass of the wasteland and the house walls of Helmouth. In the corner of the window, a fat spider squatted at the centre of its web.

She sighed. There was a deep rattle in her chest. She gripped Joe's hand.

'In the end, Joe, everything is old. The tent falls and rots away and all the folk wander or is dead and the acts is no more and all is forgot. All is forgot.'

She smiled. Corinna kissed her cheek.

'This is a good pal for you, my Corinna,' said Nanty.
'Yes,' said Corinna.

'Like a twin a bit, I think,' said Nanty. 'And it's good
to say he's braver than he thinks he is.'

Corinna grinned at Joe.

'I know he is.'

'You can go now, boy,' crackled Nanty Solo. 'Remember
this. This place come from them that tamed the wild
wild beasts. It come from them that listened to the
wild wild beasts inside themself. All they did was put a
tent round that and take it travellin' round and round
the world. You don't understand, of course. You are just
a boy. You have come for this day, the last of all our
days.'

'Come on, Joe Maloney,' said Corinna.

'When Nanty's gone and is in the box,' said Nanty,
'will you take a piece? Will you swallow Nanty?'

'Say yes,' said Corinna.

'Yes,' said Joe.

'You may kiss me then,' said Nanty Solo.

Corinna nudged him.

He trembled as he leaned towards the bed and kissed
her damaged cheek. She caught his hand and pulled it
to her mouth. She nibbled at the corner of his thumb-

nail and bit a piece off and swallowed it.

She cackled and wheezed.

'Bye-bye, little boy-thing,' she said. 'Bye-bye.'

Five

'It is! It is! It's Only Maloney! Only Maloney, lalalala . . .'

Cody's lot danced together to the song and howled with laughter.

'Here, tiger! Here, little tiger!'

'Walk proud,' said Corinna. 'They're nothing to do with you.'

She turned her face to them for an instant and spat. She told Joe about Nanty Solo, how there had been great pains in her head one year, how doctors had opened her head and taken something out, how she had been left blind, how Nanty had wept and said they had taken out her soul. She told him about the rumours: Hackenschmidt had opened her up again and dropped in a new thing – some said a spider, some said a snake's tooth, some said a drop of tiger blood, some said the tears of an angel – and then closed her again and how

Nanty was much improved by this and how she could see through the white membrane on her eyes into the deepest secrets of the human heart.

Joe tried to listen. He felt his claws, his thunderous heart. He cursed his boots, his stuttering walk, his stupidity, his stupid disguise that they'd seen through so easily. He'd be mocked for ever after for this day, for all this evidence of that stupidity. He closed his eyes, saw Stanny and Joff. They crouched by a swiftly flowing stream. They smoked cigarettes. Joff sharpened a hatchet on a stone. Stanny sharpened a knife. They grinned at each other. He should have gone with them, should have taken his own hatchet beneath the motorway and through the woods and up on to the mountain. He swiped at the stupid stripes on his face. She caught his hand. She stopped him, and stood facing him, holding his two hands, there, not fifty yards away from the mocking crew.

'You're more than you think you are,' she said. 'You're more than they think you are.'

He tugged his hands away.

'I–I know I am!' he said.

His face burned. He stared at her.

'Only Maloney, lalalala . . .'

He gasped. His head rang with the voices of those who mocked him, those who said what he should be, those who said what he could be. The words struggled for life on his tongue.

'And I–I–I am more than *you* think I–am!' he stammered.

She touched his hand again, but he pulled it away.

'That's why we need your help, Joe,' she said.

'My help?'

'That's why the tiger came for you.'

He stared. He sighed. He wondered what she meant but he knew himself that the tiger had a purpose, that it had searched for him, that it had called him. And he felt the fur on his skin. He felt the heart drumming in his chest.

'We find it hard to understand,' she whispered, 'but sometimes the most important things are the most mysterious. We don't have words for them. But we need someone like you, Joe. No, we need you.'

Joe narrowed his eyes. He stared into her. He saw other worlds, other lives. He knew that Corinna had larks and tigers inside her. He knew that her mind could stretch as far as and beyond the Black Bone Crags.

'It's always been said,' she whispered, 'that when the circus comes to an end, we'll need someone to take the beasts back to the forest. Only that way will the circus be truly ended. Only that way will our hearts be truly at rest. Only that way will we be able to think of beginning again.'

'But there's no w-wild beasts.'

She said nothing. She met his eye. He nodded. He knew that there would always be wild beasts.

Suddenly, Joe's mum's voice rang out.

'Joe! Joe!'

They turned. There she was, coming from the Cut.

'Joseph!'

He saw the fright in her eyes. He wanted to run to her, be held by her, hurry back home into Helmouth with her, take the tiger off him, take the satins off him, just be ordinary Joe Maloney again.

She slowed as she came nearer.

'You left me in the night, Joe. How could you leave me in the night?'

She kept back from him.

'How could you, Joe?'

He chewed his lips. Tears filled his eyes.

'And look at you,' she said. 'What's happening, Joe?'

'H-had a dream, Mum.'

'Oh, Joe! And you couldn't have come and woke me like all the other times?'

'I found him,' said Corinna.

'Found?'

'He was—'

'And who are you?'

'Corinna. Joe's friend. Found him at dawn.'

Joe's mum stood there, unable to speak, eyes on her boy.

'Couldn't st-stop myself,' said Joe.

She came to him, held him by the shoulders.

'I'm tr-trying to . . .'

'To what, Joseph?'

'To . . . grow up, Mum.'

'Are you, Joe? Is that what this is?'

The song started again, ringing across the wasteland towards them.

'Only Maloney, lalalala!'

'Leave him alone,' she whispered, without turning. 'Joe Maloney's worth a field full of you.'

She held him, touched the painted face.

'You did this?' she said to Corinna.

'Yes.'

Joe's mum shook her head.

'A funny'n. Such a funny'n.'

'He's fine,' said Corinna. 'I'm looking after him.'

Joe stood straight, held his head up.

'Don't need l-looking after. I'm f-fine. And I'll just be here, beside the t—'

'Tent,' said his mum. She sighed. 'You gave me such a fright.'

She blinked, asked the question of herself.

'Is this OK? Is this what should be happening when a boy grows?' The song about her son rang out again. 'Listen to them. Silly stunted stupid things. Is that what he should grow like?'

She held her boy at arm's length.

'No,' she whispered. 'He should grow like Joe Maloney, good and true.'

'I'll c-come back, Mum. I'm not going aw-away.'

They looked at each other, the three of them.

'Let me st-stay,' said Joe.

His mum lifted her eyes, scanned the tent and the billboards and the empty morning sky.

'Such a worry,' she said. 'You were always such a worry. Knew from the start there'd be strife and struggle and—'

'Clear off, circus filth!' yelled Cody's lot. 'Take your tent somewhere else!'

There was another group, too, Bleak Winters' lot. They clustered in another part of the wasteland.

'Circus equals cruelty!' they chanted. 'Set the animals free!'

'This happens everywhere you go?' said Joe's mum.

Corinna nodded.

Joe's mum gazed at the tent.

'It's a lovely thing, isn't it?' she said.

'Yes,' said Corinna.

Joe's mum held him.

'This boy walks in darkness,' she said. 'He walks where others wouldn't dare to go.'

Corinna nodded.

'You'll stay with him?'

'Yes,' said Corinna.

'Go on, then, Joe.' She cuddled her son. 'This is a girl with a heart that might be big as yours. Stay with her.'

'Yes,' he said.

'And don't forget. I'm just over there.' She smiled sadly, bright-eyed. 'Bring Corinna for lunch, Joe. Bring your new friend for lunch!'

She kissed Joe and turned away.

Corinna lifted the flap of the tent.

Six

It seemed higher, much higher than before. The faded sun and moon and stars seemed a thousand miles away. The roof of the tent reeled like the sky and Joe crouched, and pressed his hands to the straw and sawdust as if to secure himself.

She giggled.

'Second thoughts?'

'No.' He tried to steady his heart, steady his breath. 'No.'

'Come on, then.'

She took off her mac and dropped it to the floor.

'Wait here, watch me, then you do it. OK?'

She stepped up on to the rope-ladder that hung from the central pole. He saw how her feet curved over the rungs, how she could grip with her toes, saw how strong the slender muscles in her arms and legs were.

She set off climbing, then paused.

'It's easy,' she said. 'Just like falling. It'll look like miles, but the net'll catch you and hold you and you won't hurt yourself. OK?'

He nodded.

'When you've done it once, you'll want to do it again, straight away. You will, Joe.'

She climbed again, past the safety-net, until she reached the platform, and stood there.

'Nothing can happen,' she said. Her voice rang in the still blue air. 'You jump straight out like you're going to fly. You arch your body. You stretch your arms. You try to make your body beautiful and elegant and stream-lined. But even if you drop like a scared turkey, the net'll catch you and hold you. OK?'

'OK.'

She jumped, head up, body arched, arms stretched out like she was reaching for the sun and moon and stars. He watched. He wanted to copy her, but also to catch the moment when there was nothing of her to see, the moment when she disappeared. But she didn't disappear. She rolled in the air, drew her knees to her chest, landed on her shoulders, and the net sighed as it took her and held her safe.

She swung down to the sawdust beside him.

'You were . . . there all the time,' he said.

'Course I was. I'm not good enough. It's only in my dreams that *I* disappear.'

He toed the sawdust.

'But mebbe Joe Maloney's a natural, and soon's he starts jumping he starts to disappear.'

She grinned.

'Just one way to find out.'

She knelt down and started to unlace his left boot.

He stepped back.

'You think you'll go flying with these on, Joe?'

She caught his foot again. She eased the heavy boot over his heel. Joe blushed at the smell of his sweat. But she just smiled and took the sock off, too. Black dirt beneath the toenails and a rim of black around his ankle.

'Lovely feet, Joe,' she said.

Joe smiled.

She took off the other boot and sock. She rubbed his feet tenderly.

'Fancy keeping lovely little feet locked up in those things.'

She took her slippers off and stood with her feet side by side with his.

'We could nearly be t-twins,' he said.

'Ha! Yes, we could.'

Then she knelt and eased her slippers on to his feet.

'Better, eh? Much lighter. Things you can fly in.'

He flexed his toes, stood on tiptoe.

'Lovely,' he whispered.

'Up you go. Go on.'

The ladder twisted, swung and trembled as he climbed. He scrambled his way through the net.

'You're a *bit* like a turkey,' she said. 'But go on. Just go on.'

He tried to fix his eyes on the roof of the tent but he had to keep looking down at his clumsy feet on the narrow rungs, and Corinna was further and further away. Then the larks inside him started singing, helped to lift him to the platform's edge. He climbed on to it, and stood there, gripping the pole. His knees shuddered.

He looked down through the blue shade to her upturned blue face. Her eyes shone. All around, the blue starred tent wheeled.

'Listen, Joe. Look straight out, into the air above the net.'

He looked out.

'Nothing can harm you, Joe. There's just air, and that can't hurt you, and then the net'll catch you and keep you safe.'

He tried to breathe deeply, slowly.

'Mebbe it's true, Joe. Mebbe in another life, in the life before the last life, you were the greatest flier of us all.'

The larks inside him hung high in the blue and sang and sang.

'Mebbe we were together, Joe. Mebbe we were twins in sparkling costumes, catching each other high in the air while tigers growled below us.'

He teetered at the edge. He heard the awful growl, the roar, like something from some deep dark cavern rather than from an open mouth. His head reeled. He looked down and saw tigers caged inside the ring, tigers clawing the air, tigers clawing at their trainers.

'Believe in it, Joe. Just jump.'

He jumped. He held his arms out. He reached for the sun. He crumpled into the net.

He lay twisted and awkward, the net cords digging at his skin.

'Brilliant!' said Corinna, from below him. 'Brilliant, Joe.'

He rolled clumsily towards the edge of the net.

And then the air inside the tent trembled. The flap was drawn back. Hackenschmidt stood there, a huge shadow, a silhouette.

Seven

For many moments, Hackenschmidt just stared. Then he came forward, into the blue light. He wore blue trousers, a blue shirt with white flowers on it, shiny black shoes. His hair and beard were combed. He seemed three times as high as Joe, three times as wide. His arms were as broad as Joe's waist. His hands were bigger than Joe's head. He walked to Joe, who lay still at the edge of the net.

'Come down,' he said. His voice was soft and calm. He lifted Joe with his great hands from the net. He slowly swung him down on to the sawdust floor. He straightened Joe's satin clothes, just as Joe's mother would. 'Do you know who I am?' he asked.

'H-Hack—'

'Yes. Hackenschmidt. The Lion of Russia, the greatest wrestler ever seen. The champion of the world. The . . .'

His voice faltered and he sighed. 'And you are Joe Maloney.'

'Yes,' said Joe.

'You'll refresh the world, you and my Corinna.'

He turned his eyes to the trapeze.

'You went up there, eh?'

'Yes.'

'Brave boy.'

He sighed again. His breath fell across Joe's face. They stood together, the huge man, the scrawny boy, the lithe girl. They stood in the blue shade, in deep silence, just the sighing of breath, distant drone of traffic, the shifting of the tent.

'Listen to it,' whispered Hackenschmidt at last. 'The lovely gentle sound of canvas between the world in here and the world out there. Do you think it's lovely, Joe?'

'Yes.'

They gazed towards the ancient faded galaxy. They breathed the blue air and the dust.

'Soon,' said Hackenschmidt, 'the tent will be gone. Everything that has happened in here . . .' He flicked his fingers at the air. 'Gone, just like that.'

Great sadness crossed his face.

'We have been so beautiful, Joe. Even me, even ugly Hackenschmidt. So beautiful.'

He smiled, and was silent for a long time, and Joe watched him, and relaxed, and knew that once again he had found a stranger who was also familiar.

'I don't have many words,' said Hackenschmidt. 'I grunt and growl and howl. My body has been my expression all these years.'

Silence again. Hackenschmidt lowered his eyes.

'Step on to my hands,' he whispered.

He knelt and spread his two hands flat before Joe's feet.

'Go on,' said Hackenschmidt. 'Step on to them. Stand still. Trust me, Joe.'

Joe stepped forward and stood on the great palms.

'Imagine you're part of me,' said Hackenschmidt. 'Imagine you grew out of me.'

Joe breathed deeply as Hackenschmidt lifted him. He tottered, and he reached out to Hackenschmidt's shoulders, but the hands beneath his feet tilted and shifted in order to keep him in balance.

'Trust me,' said Hackenschmidt.

Joe relaxed. He rose higher. He felt how Hackenschmidt responded to him, supported him, understood him. Hackenschmidt lowered him again, laid him on the floor again.

'We'll let no harm come to you,' he said.

Joe breathed calmly.

'The tiger came for you,' said Hackenschmidt.

'Yes.'

'Did you see me as well? In the darkness, between the houses and the wasteland. Did you see me there?'

Joe spun back into his dream. He stood at the window, stared out at the massive figure in the Cut.

'Did you hear me?' said Hackenschmidt. 'Tiger! Tiger!'

'Yes,' said Joe. 'I thought I was as–asleep, but . . .'

'Me too. I snuffled and snored through it all, Joe Maloney. You saw Hackenschmidt, but there was no Hackenschmidt. Hackenschmidt was in his dreams.'

Joe sighed. He closed his eyes. He brought to mind the tiger, the glittering eyes, the hot, sour breath, the harsh tongue, the great curved teeth. He looked at Hackenschmidt, at Corinna.

'I . . . I saw you. I saw the t–tiger.'

'Yes. Hackenschmidt was in the dream of Joe Maloney. Joe Maloney was in the dream of Hackenschmidt. The tiger was the one that prowled between us, the thing that crossed from dream to dream. The tiger was the one that found you out and brought you to me. You understand?' Hackenschmidt shook his head. 'Me neither, Joe.'

Joe couldn't go on with this. He floundered. His head reeled. He closed his eyes. Skylarks burst out singing deep inside. He dreamed of being lifted from the sawdust ring, soaring through the galaxy, hanging far off in the endless blue of sky. He felt Hackenschmidt's great hands cradling his head, felt the great thumbs stroking his brow, heard the low whisper.

'Joe. Joe. Joe.'

'Where you gone?' Corinna said gently.

He came back down to earth.

Hackenschmidt held him.

'You've come home, Joe,' he breathed. 'That tiger's gone out prowling many nights, through all the wastelands and little towns we've been these past few years. Night after night I've dreamed him finding nothing, nobody. He's prowled through simple total darkness, seen by no one. Till now. Till you.'

He smiled.

'The tiger brought you home, Joe. I'm so happy that we found you. Now show me what you did.'

'Eh?'

'Climb up again. Jump again. Go on.'

'Go on, Joe,' said Corinna. 'We think he was mebbe a flier in another life, Hackenschmidt. We think mebbe he and me was together.'

'Yes. That's possible. That would explain a great deal.' He held Joe's shoulders. 'You don't remember it, though?'

'N–No.'

'Ah, well. Go on up.'

Joe climbed. Hackenschmidt held the ladder tight beneath him. He climbed through the net, to the platform. Stood there, clinging to the pole. Stared into the empty air that could do no harm. Tried to imagine a world with the tent gone, just empty air going on for ever and for ever. Could not imagine it. Closed his eyes and the tiger came, with its stench, its growl. Closed his eyes and the voice of Hackenschmidt came.

'We need a boy with the heart of a tiger. We need a hero. We need you, Joe.'

Joe teetered.

'Now jump!' called Hackenschmidt. 'Go on, Joe Maloney. Jump!'

He jumped. He jumped as if he jumped away from all his fears, all his confusions, as if he jumped into a world that he had searched for in all his days and nights of wandering the wasteland. He reached into the air as if nothing would ever stop him, as if he'd go on jumping for ever more.

The net sighed and creaked. Joe rolled to the edge. There was only Corinna below. No Hackenschmidt, as if he'd never been there at all.

Eight

Corinna giggled as she pulled Joe's clumsy boots on to her feet and stood up and did an awkward dance in them.

'When I was little,' she said, 'he taped silver slippers round my feet. "Dance, dance, dance," he said. I could barely walk. My first memory – standing here, his voice going, "Dance, dance, dance." '

'Hackenschmidt?'

'Hackenschmidt.'

They sat on the low wooden wall around the ring. Sunlight through the canvas walls intensified. Far-off traffic din. Vague bitter chanting from outside.

'He used to lift me up and throw me through the air. He flipped me into somersaults and cartwheels. He held metal bars and told me to jump up and swing from them. Hoops to dive through, ropes to climb, rings to swing from. All the time: "Corinna, Corinna, do it, Corinna. Now this. Now this. Jump for this, Corinna. Dive over this. Be graceful as the swallow, brave as the tiger, strong as the bear . . ." It was him that turned me into what I am.'

'Not your m—?'

She shook her head.

'I remember her standing at the tent door, standing still and silent and looking in at us. But mostly it's just me and Hackenschmidt.' She shrugged. 'Mebbe she lost interest straight away, once she saw I wasn't good enough.'

'But you're br—'

'Brilliant! I wish . . .'

She toed the dust with her bare feet.

'When you were little here in Helmouth, I was little in this tent, travelling and travelling. D'you think something linked us even then?'

'Eh?'

'There was always something missing. I could feel myself yearning for something. Like Nanty said – for a twin, mebbe. Somebody to be with that was like myself. You must've felt that, Joe.'

Joe nodded.

'Yes. I f-felt that.'

'This hasn't just happened,' she said. 'We know each other from . . .'

'L–long long ago.'

She toed the sawdust. A pot-bellied pig shoved in through the door and wandered towards them.

'Hello, Little Fatty,' she said, and the pig snuffled and grunted.

'We had the unicorns then, when I was small,' she said.

'Unicorns?'

'You saw them on Nanty Solo's wall. They were secret.'

She reached out to the pig and let it nuzzle her fingers. Joe thought of his own unicorns. He'd known them since he too was small. He'd seen them in his dreams, roaming the Silver Forest.

'We couldn't let them out,' she said. 'They used to wander about in here, jump on the seats, scamper about the ring. Lovely things, just like you, Little Fatty.'

'Where did you g—?'

'Get them from?' She shrugged. 'Oh, they were lovely, but not real. They were white goats from Andalucia. When they were still babies, Hackenschmidt took out their two horn buds and replaced just one at the middle of their brows.'

The pig licked and Corinna giggled.

'And they gr—?' said Joe.

'You saw them. They grew like the single horns of

unicorns. Some of them were all twisted but a couple grew straight out just like they should. No teeth, Fatty! They were going to be an act. They were something to stop the circus going from bad to worse. But the cruelty people found out. So we kept them hidden. Sweet as angels. Fatty!'

Joe looked around him, imagined gentle unicorns scampering there, heard their bleats and whimpers. Things that weren't supposed to be, things that lived just in dreams and stories. The pig nuzzled his little feet.

'Fatty!' laughed Corinna. She smiled at Joe. 'There were tales that some circus somewhere had done it to children – put horn buds into the brows of babies to turn them into fauns. We had a clown once that said he'd seen them – the fauns – performing in a village in Romania.'

Fauns. Joe knew these as well. Half beast, half human, glimpsed as they crossed the shadows between the trees.

'Sometimes I dream that Hackenschmidt did it to me,' she said. 'I wake up touching my brow, and expect to find horns there.'

She drew her hair back.

'See anything?'

Joe looked. He shook his head. He touched her brow tenderly with his fingers. Nothing, just smooth unbroken speckled skin stretched across her skull.

'Nothing,' he said.

'He put the unicorns down a couple of years back,' she went on. 'Drowned them. Said it was better that way. They were out of place in this harsh world. Mebbe their spirits would find somewhere better if he freed them.' She stroked the pig. 'Mebbe there's a little lovely world close by that's filled with unicorns and fauns. What d'you think, Fatty?'

The pig licked, grunted, and nuzzled her.

'Aye,' she said. 'And with little fat pigs as well.'

And she stepped up, arched her body, spun in cartwheels round the ring, while Joe closed his eyes, and fingered his brow, feeling for scars and ridges and lumps. He dreamed of horns growing there, dreamed of being a creature in another world close by, or of living in someone else's dream or story. This is me, he thought, a half-beast, half-human thing, a thing that can sprout horns or fur or feathers.

Corinna came to rest in front of him.

'Deep in the circus there's a secret heart,' she said.

Joe stared.

'Secret?'

'In the circus, and in yourself. That's what we're moving towards.'

Joe just stared again.

'We're moving towards your secret heart. I have to take you to it. That's why the tiger came.'

Joe stared back at her.

'We'll need you all night, Joe. Can you stay all night?'

Nine

The kids at the Cut moved across the entrance to block the path. They held tins of lager loosely in their fists. They tilted their heads to the side and breathed out plumes of smoke. Mac Bly threw his arms about as if in panic. George Carr screamed about the tigers coming. Jug Matthews whistled at Corinna's legs and scoffed at her boots.

'Lock your kids up quick!' said Goldie Wills. 'The freaks is out.'

Joe and Corinna kept on walking. They sidled through the group, through the shoving shoulders and jutting elbows. Voices whispered in contempt. Eyes leered and challenged. Scents of alcohol, tobacco smoke, dope. The song was sung, soft and threatening,

'Only Maloney, lalalala . . .'

The words were coarse and cruel:

'In with the Gyppos now, Maloney? In with the

wasters and wanderers and tramps and thieves? Found your proper place, eh? Only place where Only isn't Only, eh?'

But Joe also heard traces of wonder in the voices, traces of fear in the reeling eyes.

'Get . . . out . . . the way,' he stammered.

'Ooooh! Maloney's getting mad!'

'Yes,' hissed Corinna. 'Get out our bloody way.'

'And the Gyppo fairy tart as well.'

Goldie danced around Corinna with her fists raised.

'Come on, then, Gyppo fairy tart,' she said. 'Come on. Take us on.'

'Chicken, they're both bloody chicken!' laughed Plug and all the others, and they squawked and bobbed and pushed their elbows back like stupid stunted birds.

They got through. Curses and whispers and the song followed them.

Corinna brushed her body as if brushing off dirt.

'That's what all kids is like out here?' she spat.

Joe shrugged.

'That's who you live among?' she snapped.

'Lost souls!' she hissed. 'Lost souls! Lost souls!'

She spat and rubbed her spit into the dust with her boot.

They entered the street of pale houses. Dust in the gutters and in the cracks on the pavements. Rampant hedges. Little kids played around a garden gate, jumping an elastic band they'd stretched there. They stood in astonishment as the tiger-faced boy and the girl dressed for the trapeze approached them. Their wide eyes shone. They reached out to touch the pair as they passed by. Corinna paused, and reached down to tousle their hair.

'Mebbe not all of them is lost, then,' she said.

She jumped with them across their band, so graceful.

'Do this,' she said, stretching her arms wide as she jumped, pointing her toes, tilting her head. 'Or this. Or this.'

The children watched, and the bravest of them copied her.

'That's right,' she said. 'Oh, that's wonderful. Think of birds, think of fairies, think of angels. Let the pictures in your mind take shape in your bodies. That's lovely. Oh, that's wonderful! Wow, you're brilliant!'

They walked on, leaving their images to stroll for years afterwards in the children's minds.

They paused at the gate.

'My h—' said Joe.

There was a long jagged crack in the pebbledash by the door. There was a single hawthorn tree that Joe's mum had planted when he was born. The garden was thistles and weeds and wild flowers where bees buzzed and a pair of red butterflies flew. This was where Joe

123

used to crawl as a baby while his mum sat on the front step watching. She used to hug him when he crawled back out with jabbered tales of rabbits and elves and fairies. She used to take him on her knee and laugh as she listened. 'Is that right?' she used to say. 'Is that really what you saw in there? Well, I never!'

Joe breathed deeply. She'd always wanted him to bring a friend home.

'C-come in,' he said.

To the back of the house, the back garden, an overgrown lawn with more weeds and wild flowers growing. At the centre, Mum lay on a sun lounger and wore a swimsuit and sunglasses. Music poured out of a little radio, Tina Turner, her favourite. There was a tray with an emptied glass and plate. 'Mum!' Joe said. 'Mum.' But Tina Turner drowned him out. He remembered crawling here also, crawling as far as the high back fence where he found real toads, real spiders, where he heard fairies and pixies whispering and singing into his ear. Then toddling quickly back to her open arms with his tales again.

Joe didn't move. She looked so lovely, so relaxed there, letting the sun pour down on her from the unblemished sky. Already he felt older, much older than he had last night.

'Mum,' he said. 'Mum.'

Too softly.

'She looks lovely,' said Corinna.

'Y-yes. Mum!'

A breeze blew through the garden and she stirred. She brushed a wasp away from her face. She sat up and turned and lifted the sunglasses from her eyes. She looked at him as if there was no disguise, as if she saw straight through to her Joe.

'Hello, Joe. And Corinna, too. Come on, then, before I have to dash off for my shift.'

She wrapped a gown around her and came smiling towards them.

'Now then, Corinna,' she said. 'Come on. Come in. There's not a lot but what we've got you're welcome to.'

Ten

They sat on stools at the kitchen table. They ate cheese and tomatoes and the sun shone bright through the kitchen window. Corinna looked around herself in fascination.

'Never been in a house before,' she said.

'Never?' said Joe's mum.

'No. Never. Just caravans and tents. Been in shops and pubs sometimes, but never a house.'

Joe looked at the room with new eyes, thought of all the rooms around them, the roof protecting them from the sky, the foundations dug deep into the ground.

'Always wondered what they was like inside,' she said. 'The walls is thick, eh?'

Joe and his mum just looked at each other and laughed.

'Funny to be in something that never moves,' Corinna said.

She stamped gently on the floor. She reached out and tapped the flowered wallpaper. She shook her head at the strangeness of it. She chewed her bread and cheese. Joe's mum watched her with pleasure.

'You know,' she said, 'you look lovely. Your costume and everything. Doesn't she, Joe?'

Joe blushed and nodded.

'I'd've liked to be something like you. Light and easy and free, swinging on the trapeze. I bet you're good.'

'She's brill—' said Joe.

'No, I'm not,' said Corinna.

'I used to do it in the garden when I was little,' said Joe's mum. Her eyes shone as she remembered. 'Isn't that funny? I'd nearly forgot about that. We had a cherry tree and I swung and swung and swung all day and me mam used to yell out the house, "Are you never coming off that blinking swing?" '

She laughed.

'Kids, eh? Dreams and games and heads that turn little gardens into whole new worlds. And what about your mam and dad, Corinna?'

'Mum's in Russia. Dad . . . Well, nobody knows about my dad.'

'Ah, well, that's the way for many these days. No brothers, no sisters?'

'No brothers, no sisters.'

'But a tent full of friends.'

'Yes. And a new friend. Joe Maloney.'

'That's right. Here, Corinna. You seen his pictures?'

She pointed to Joe's pictures on the walls. Faded paper, dried-out and curled. Faded paints. Pictures from the days he used to crawl away from her through the weeds, pictures from when he came running back from outside the village with tales of visions and wonders. Clumsy crayon pictures of creatures with wings and horns.

'They're good, eh?' said his mum.

'Brilliant,' said Corinna.

She touched Joe's hand.

'They're brilliant,' she said.

Joe shrugged.

'From l—'

'From long ago. They're brilliant.'

Joe's mum looked at her watch.

'Got to go soon,' she said. 'Be selling booze in half an hour. So what's the plan for the rest of the day? You going to turn into a trapeze artist, Joe Maloney?' She smiled at his painted face. 'Or are they putting you in a cage?'

'Tiger tamer.' He laughed.

'Starting at the top, eh? I thought you told me there was no tigers.'

'Oh, there's d–dozens.'

'Well, no putting your head in their mouths, at least for the first day.'

'OK, Mum.'

She stroked his head.

'You look after yourself over there. And no getting in anybody's way.'

'OK, Mum.' He licked his lips. 'Mum . . .'

'Yes, love?'

'Could I st–stay all night?'

'So this is what you're plotting, Joe Maloney? This is why you brought your new pal?'

Joe shrugged.

'We've been showing him it all,' said Corinna. 'The trapeze and the dogs and everything. It'd be great. Everybody likes him.'

Mum pondered.

'We're all right, you know,' said Corinna. 'We're not what some folk say.'

'Oh, don't worry. I know that, pet. Not like some round here.'

She touched Joe's hair.

'It's what you want, eh?'

Joe nodded. She looked through the window towards the wall of the tent, the blue slope against the blue sky.

'I can see it's your kind of thing.' She smiled.

'Should've heard some of the notions he had as a bairn. And still has.' She sighed and pondered and assessed Corinna. 'You're a good lass,' she said. 'Listen, Joseph Maloney. You listen to Corinna. OK?'

'OK.'

She picked up her keys from the table.

'Mum,' said Joe.

'Eh?'

He wanted to tell her about the tiger, about Hackenschmidt and Nanty Solo. He wanted to tell her that he'd already changed and that by the time she'd see him again he'd have changed again. But he stammered and sighed and just looked at her.

She smiled, so gentle. 'Come here,' she said. She held him tight beside the kitchen table. 'What a great boy I've brought into this world.'

Joe laughed softly.

'You be careful,' she said.

'Yes.'

'And I want you reporting back first thing in the morning, right?'

'Right.'

'Don't want you getting eaten by them tigers, do we?'

'No,' said Joe. 'No, Mum.'

Eleven

Joe and Corinna stood by the tent and looked across the motorway towards the Black Bone Crags. Inside, the afternoon performance was already going on. By now new posters had been hung on the tent and plastered on the billboards: LAST DAY, LAST DAY, LAST DAY. Already the audience was laughing at Wilfred and his dogs. The sun had passed its centre, and was heading slowly down towards the western edge of the earth again. Joe imagined Stanny and Joff out there, invisible beings in the great landscape that swept away from Helmouth. Tonight a tiny spark of flame, a tiny wisp of smoke, would mark their place out there. Moths would be drawn to it, and greater creatures, dark shadows blooming from the dark of night. He shuddered. He saw Joff's thumb stroke the hatchet blade, saw the tiny bulbs of blood rising on the skin. He raised his eyes towards the sky above the crags.

'You . . . s–see them?'

He stretched his arm out, stretched his index finger.

'See what, Joe?'

'They fly.'

He moved his finger, following their flight. Tiny things, so far away. Tiny things that even his mother had never admitted seeing.

'Birds?' said Corinna. 'Eagles or something?'

Joe slowly shook his head and pointed and watched.

'Not birds?' she said.

They spiralled upward from the crags.

'What are they, Joe?'

Joe shrugged. One day he'd seen Bleak Winters with binoculars in the yard at Hangar's High. A first-year jumped beside him, pointed insistently towards the sky. 'Please, sir. Please, sir. Look properly. They're there! They're really there!' Bleak laughed. He lowered the binoculars and grinned. Crows, buzzards, eagles, nothing, empty air. He snorted, cuffed the first-year's shoulder. 'Silly boy. Dreamer.'

Corinna leaned against Joe, pressed her head close to his, as if to see through his eyes.

'I see them, but . . .'

'You s–see them?'

They had flown all through his infancy, beating their wings against the distant blue, beating their wings through his dreams. As a baby in his pushchair, as Mum pushed him by the Blood Pond or alongside the Lostleg Railway, he used to raise his podgy finger. 'What d'you see?' she used to murmur, crouching and looking into his excited yearning eyes. 'What do you see out there? Ah, if only you had the words to tell me, Joe.'

'You see them?' he said again to his new friend.

'Yes, but . . . Not birds,' said Corinna. 'What are they, Joe?'

Joe gripped her hand, stared, stammered, shook his head. He didn't know what they were, just knew that they existed there, at the furthest highest fringes of his mind, that they flew between the edge of earth and the edge of sky. He shivered with the sudden joy of them, the sudden joy he'd known ever since his infancy every time they showed themselves to him. He tilted his head upwards, closed his eyes, and knew the extra joy of standing there with another who saw them, too.

'Cor-inna,' he whispered. 'Corinna. You s-see.'

'Yes,' she said.

'And h-hear?'

He tilted his head to the side, caught the weird whisperings and murmurings, like sweet noises from creatures so close, so close.

'Hear?' she said.

And she too tilted her head like Joe did. She looked

into his eyes, leaned close to him, tried to hear with his ears.

'Noises,' she whispered.

'Yes.'

'Yes. Like . . . like animals. But not like animals. Like . . .'

'Y—'

'Birds?'

'Yes. Sk–skylarks.'

She gasped and her eyes suddenly widened, and Joe knew that the larks screamed inside her as they did in him, that they raged inside her heart, that they raised her spirit from the battered earth of Helmouth.

'Cor-inna,' he said. 'Corinna!'

Then came a great roar, a howl of hate and anguish.

'Hackenschmidt,' said Corinna. 'They're putting him in the cage already. Come on, I have to be quick.'

Twelve

Joe sat on a stool inside the entrance to the performers' tunnel. Corinna sat by him tying on new spangled slippers.

Charley Caruso came. He gazed into Joe's tiger's face and breathed,

'Tomasso! Tomasso!'

Joe shook his head and Charley raised his hands in apology and sorrow.

Then Wilfred, with a tiny dog in his arms. 'You're Joe, aren't you?' he said, in his sweet shy voice.

Joe nodded.

'Brave boy,' said Wilfred. 'Beautiful brave boy.'

Then he hugged Corinna.

'The last day,' he said. 'What will come to us afterwards?'

She shrugged and sighed.

'We have each other,' said Wilfred. 'Maybe we'll find

a little world for funny folk like us and we'll picnic there together the rest of our lives.'

He smiled and kissed the little dog.

'Oh, it's a cruel world we live in, Nellie, a cruel cruel world.'

Further back, Hackenschmidt sat on the floor of his cage in silence.

Inside the ring, a clown dressed in a yellow Stetson pretended to ride Little Fatty like a wild horse. Another poured buckets of water into his trousers, then threw a bucket of shredded paper into the crowd.

The sparse crowd lounged on the benches and was bored.

Older kids from the estate flexed their muscles and slapped and punched each other.

'Get the wild man on!' they yelled. 'Bring the bloody beast out!'

There were others who'd come for the fight, silent men who stared into the ring and dreamed the moves they'd make to catch out Hackenschmidt and make a thousand pounds.

After the clowns, Corinna caught her breath, stood on tiptoe, then skipped past Joe into the ring. She climbed towards the summit. She danced on ropes and swings. She stretched her arms out wide and crossed the high wire to a drum roll from below. She held out her arms like the wings of a bird. She smiled at Joe. She waved.

'Gerroff!' they yelled. 'Bring the wild man on!'

She dived into the sighing net to a scatter of applause and hurried back to Joe.

'You were br—' he said.

'I wasn't. And even if I was, they wouldn't know.'

She glared into the tent. The crowd yelled and chanted for Hackenschmidt.

'Don't want to see this,' she said. 'Let's go out, Joe.'

She reached into the cage as Hackenschmidt was wheeled past them. He took her hand and reached out for Joe's.

'Not long till dusk,' he said. 'Run about. Be children. Enjoy yourselves.'

Corinna touched his face tenderly. She kissed his hand.

'Don't worry,' he told her.

'Oh, Hackenschmidt. Let them be careful with you.'

He nodded sadly, dipped his fingers into a bowl of bloody liquid, and striped it on his face. As Joe and Corinna left him, he was already howling, the crowd was baying for his blood.

Thirteen

Sky was darkening. The sun a massive orange ball. Orange wisps of clouds above the crags. Shadows lengthening on the Golden Mountain, darkness deepening in the Silver Forest. They moved quickly, past the posters:

HACKENSCHMIDT'S CIRCUS.
THE FINAL TOUR.
YOUR FINAL CHANCE.
NEVER TO BE SEEN AGAIN.
LAST DAY, LAST DAY, LAST DAY, LAST DAY

They passed the billboards: Hackenschmidt in his astounding youth; savage animals in a pretty English glade. She took his hand and led him between the desolate caravans. They passed Nanty Solo's place and saw her there, inside the window, sitting up in her bed.

She turned her sightless eyes and smiled as they passed by.

'Where do we go?' asked Corinna.

Joe stared.

'You're the one that knows this place, Joe.'

Joe laughed. He gripped her hand and pulled her forward. Their feet quickened on the slope. They stumbled on the tussocky grass, fell headlong over stones and fallen walls, tumbled into potholes left by ancient cellars. They laughed at each other, picked themselves up and ran again. Joe tried to talk, tried to name these places he knew so well, but his voice in its excitement leaped into wordless gabbles and whoops. He took her down through the Blessed Chapel, where he knelt with her by the broken stones. Joe breathed,

'Sp–spirits of the ear–earth and air pro–protect my mum.'

Corinna knelt beside him.

'S–say the words,' said Joe.

'Spirits of the earth and air . . .'

'That's right,' said Joe.

'Look after Hackenschmidt and Joe Maloney and me tonight.'

She bobbed her head urgently a few times.

'Now this,' he said.

He showed her how to spit on her hands and wipe

them slowly across the name of God. He showed her how to pick dirt and sprinkle it on her tongue, how to lick the moisture of moss.

He snapped a button from his shirt and dropped it through the narrow slot between the stones.

Howls of anger echoed from the tent.

Corinna bobbed her head and bobbed her head and begged protection. Then she, too, snapped off a button and dropped it through the slot.

They stood again and ran again, down Adder Lane, across the Ratty Paddocks, past the Blood Pond that deepened in its redness as the sun went down. The motorway grumbled and flashed. Above the distant Black Bone Crags, the creatures flapped again. He led her to the Hag's Kitchen, fed her clover and mushrooms and thistle nuts, and he danced for her, free as never before in his satin and his slippers and the stripes of tiger on his face. And Corinna laughed and danced with him and howled a noise to drown the howls that still caught up with them, even at this distance from the tent.

Then they lay on the turf in silence, and there was silence all around. The sun's last fiery edge peeped above the crags, then was gone. She was a shadow at his side, here in the wasteland. He turned his head to her.

'It's tr-true,' he said. 'I knew you from l—'

'Long ago.'

They trembled and sighed together as the stars above intensified.

'We must go back,' whispered Corinna at last.

They began to retrace their steps uphill. They were dazed, stunned, stupefied.

From far behind them came the roar, the high-pitched yell of fear, anger, pain. The scream of an animal. It echoed across the slopes, across the motorway, across the ruined fringes of Helmouth. It echoed into their hearts and beyond their hearts.

They stopped, stared across towards the Golden Hills.

'Cruel cruel world,' whispered Corinna.

Joe groaned. He saw sharpened steel, bulbs of blood, streams of blood. He felt steel on skin, on flesh, on bone. He heard harsh laughter. The deep dark caverns inside himself began to open.

Joe and Corinna walked uphill again. Above them, the first stars began to show themselves. The first lights of Helmouth began to sparkle, like a sky upon the earth. They walked in silence towards the blue tent, two slender creatures, twins.

Fourteen

There were small fires being lit around the tent, in the spaces between the caravans. The scent of burning wood, of meat held on forks close to the crackling flames. Faces glowed like lanterns. They turned to Joe and Corinna as they passed. Murmured greetings and blessings accompanied them. Somewhere children sang songs passed down from early days: laments for lost loves, lullabies, songs to pacify the fairies and ghosts that inhabit the night. From inside the estate came a noise of celebration: mocking cries and chants, yells of triumph. Joe's heart trembled in its secret place. He looked across the wasteland to the bright red sign, **BOOZE BIN**, and saw his mum in there wrapping tins and bottles. Felt the urge to run to her, to hold her again, but didn't run. Kept walking with Corinna at his side.

A simple notice hung across the entrance to the tent:

FINISHED. NO MORE.

Corinna held the flap aside. She took deep breaths.

'Come back in,' she said.

Candles burned, as they must have in the first days. They were sparsely scattered about the benches. The clowns climbed among the benches, lighting more in distant areas of dark. High above, the galaxy softly glowed. The canvas was dead still and blue as dusk. Hackenschmidt lay at the centre of the ring. Wilfred and Charley Caruso knelt at his side. They had bowls of water and cloths that they cleaned and soothed him with. Nanty Solo sat cross-legged at their side, whispering, murmuring, singing.

Corinna clicked her tongue and sighed.

'Come on,' she said, tugging Joe forward. 'See what they've done, these people you live with?'

She glared into his eyes.

'He never harmed a soul, and look what they've bloody done to him!'

'Leave him alone,' whispered Hackenschmidt. He smiled through his pain. 'It is what they were supposed to do, after all.'

He winced and groaned. There were cuts and bruises all across his face. The savage marks of boot soles and fists. A ring of bitter red around his throat.

'They'd have killed him,' said Wilfred. 'We had to drag them off. Had to say if they killed him there'd be no cash. Swine.'

Nanty muttered strings of words:

'The last day, on the last of all days . . .'

Hackenschmidt reached out to Joe.

'Was easy for them in the end, boy. Easy to beat Hackenschmidt. Just wait for the day he says he's had enough, then get kicking.'

'Seven of them in the end,' said Wilfred. 'Others at the fringes waiting to jump in. And the crowd baying and laughing. "Get stuck in!" Even while they were going out, already fighting over how to split the thousand quid. Bloody swine.'

Charley put his arm around Joe's shoulder.

'Ah, Tomasso,' he whispered. 'What are we come to, my Tomasso?'

Hackenschmidt licked the blood that trickled from his lips.

He smiled.

'Help me up, Joe.'

He stretched out his great hand. Joe took it, felt the great weight of Hackenschmidt as he raised himself painfully from the floor.

'Good lad,' whispered Hackenschmidt. 'Aren't we lucky to have found a boy like you in a place like this?'

'It was meant to be,' said Corinna.

'Yes,' said Hackenschmidt. 'Not luck. It was always meant to be.'

They all sat together on the sawdust floor beneath the twinkling candles, and they leaned close to Nanty Solo as she began to speak.

Fifteen

'In the deepest of the deep, in the darkest of the dark,' she said, 'there lived a tiger. Ah, it was a thing of tale and rumour. An impossible thing of stripes and cruel cold eyes and great curved teeth and claws and a tongue that could lick flesh and skin from bone. It was longer than the length of a man and higher than the height of a boy. Such a creature, a creature of the foulest terror and the finest beauty, could surely not exist. It padded only through the tales brought back into this world by ancient travellers. It lived alongside their dragons, their sea monsters and unicorns. It prowled only in our dreams, only in the hidden corners of our minds. It roared deep inside our secret hearts. We did not expect to see this thing, even though we had come to love it, even though we were terrified by it. Paltry souls, we could not imagine the power of the earth and the air and the seas and the sun to bring such a creature into being.'

She smiled, and reached out to touch Joe and then Corinna, who sat each side of her.

'Then, at an unknown time on an unknown day in the distant past, one of us stepped into the forest. Who was it? Someone who understood that what we imagined could also be something that we touched. Someone who understood that as we stepped into the forest we stepped into the unknown fringes of the mind. Someone like you, Corinna. Someone like you, Joe Maloney. As you walked, you began to smell it, the hot, sour breath, the stench of its pelt. You felt the animal wildness on your tongue, in your nostrils. The tiger moved towards you through the forest, as if it knew you, as if it was drawn to you. You heard its footpads at your side. You heard its long slow breath, the sighing in its lungs, the rattle in its throat. And then it stepped out from the forest and stood across your path. The cruel eyes stared into you. The hot tongue, harsh as sandpaper, licked your arm. The mouth opened, the curved teeth were poised to close on you. You couldn't move. You prepared to die . . . But you didn't die. You stood before the tiger and you didn't die . . .'

There was movement in the darkness of the performers' tunnel. Joe looked. Nothing. Then he saw the two clowns there, holding some great burden across their arms. Corinna touched Joe's forearm tenderly. Nanty touched his hand.

'We brought the tiger out, Joe Maloney. We carried it out of the darkness into the light. We carried it across the earth. We carried it across seas and over rivers and along tracks and roads. We brought it to the open spaces beside great cities, to tiny villages beyond high hills, we brought it to places like Helmouth. And how they rushed to see this wonder! How they hurried to the great blue tent that glowed between the sky and the earth! How they shuddered! How they gasped to see this thing of dreams that had become so real! How scared they were. How overjoyed.'

Joe looked again towards the tunnel.

'You're scared,' said Nanty.

He nodded.

'Y-yes.'

'So was the tiger when it stepped out on to the path, Joe. So is the tiger now, now that it becomes once more a thing of dream and imagination and memory.'

Her white eyes glowed in the candlelight.

'The forests are almost empty of their tigers, Joe. Our secret hearts are almost empty.'

The breath rattled in her throat.

'We are paltry souls, Joe. Will we ever be able to imagine our tigers again and make them step out on to our path?'

148

Her sightless gaze rested on him. No way of answering her. He stammered. She smiled. Her touch was gentle.

'Don't worry,' she whispered. 'Yours is the bravest soul of all. The tiger has chosen you to carry it out of the glowing blue tent and into the forest again.'

Joe trembled.

The clowns moved out of the tunnel towards the ring. They laid their burden on the sawdust and unrolled it.

Sixteen

It was a tiger skin, huge and heavy and wonderful. It lay there spread out on the sawdust, the place where it had once leaped and roared and clawed the air.

Hackenschmidt sighed.

'Touch it, Joe,' he said.

Joe touched. The fur was so dense. The skin itself felt leathery, ancient. He spread out his hand beneath the pelt and lifted and felt the great weight of it.

'Isn't it beautiful?' said Corinna.

Joe nodded.

'It was the last of our tigers. Died long before I was born. We've carried it with us, always and everywhere.'

'Put it on, Joe,' said Hackenschmidt.

Joe flinched.

'Go on. Put it on.'

Joe looked up to the wheeling galaxy. He saw his mum in his room, looking down at his empty bed. He heard the cruel triumphant yells of Joff and Stanny Mole. He looked at the tiger skin, and knew that somehow he had always known that he would put it on.

Hackenschmidt lifted the skin from the floor as if it were a cape. Joe looked into the deep shadowed space between the skin and the sawdust.

'Go in there,' said Hackenschmidt.

Nanty Solo smiled. Wilfred and Charley Caruso nodded at him: yes, go in. Corinna crouched at his side.

'I'm here, Joe,' she said. 'I won't leave you.'

Joe closed his eyes. He crawled on all fours into the shadowed space. Hackenschmidt laid the tiger skin across his back. Joe sighed as his body took the weight. The pelt spread out around him, and Joe knew how puny he was compared with the creature that had once inhabited this space. The skin of the head fell down across his face. Through the eyeholes he saw the candles twinkling, Hackenschmidt looking in at him. He saw Wilfred, Charley and Nanty Solo leave the ring.

Corinna's voice:

'I'm here, Joe. I won't leave you.'

'Just breathe,' whispered Hackenschmidt. 'Just be yourself, Joe Maloney.'

Joe breathed. He hung his head. He felt the skin draped over his own skin. He waited. No one spoke.

No one moved. He waited. He waited.

The tigerness swelled, as if from that chip of bone he'd eaten all those hours ago, as if from an ancient secret darkness in his heart. It came slowly, like a vague scent carried on a breeze blowing through him, like the echo of a roar inside some distant cavern. It came closer, closer, as if it had waited always for this moment. He felt fur breaking through his skin. He felt heavy paws and lethal claws. He felt the power of his muscles, his bones. His breathing deepened, sighed from deep new lungs. He felt the heart, his tiger heart, drumming in his chest. He heard the roar that echoed from his throat. He clawed the air. He bared his massive fangs. Memories rushed through his blood, his bones, his flesh, his brain: he ran through hot grassland, with antelope running before him and other tigers running alongside him; he prowled the shadows of forests. Beneath the pelt, beneath that curious tent of skin and striped fur, Joe Maloney danced a tiger dance, was transformed by tigerness, became a tiger.

He fell to the sawdust floor. His body jerked and trembled. Hackenschmidt lifted the skin away.

'Joe,' said Corinna. 'Joe. Joe.'

She took his hand, helped him to his feet.

They stood in the flickering dark, candles and canvas

like the whole universe spinning about them. They waited. They waited.

And they heard it in the ring beside them, the footsteps, the breath. They caught the scent of its breath, its pelt. It circled them. They caught sight of it – its stripes, its glittering eyes – as it moved through the edges of their vision.

'Tiger!' said Corinna.

'On the last day,' whispered Nanty Solo. 'On the last of all days . . .'

'Go on,' said Hackenschmidt. 'Take it out.'

He went to the door and held the flap of canvas aside. Joe and Corinna went together. They stepped into the glistening night. They moved across the wasteland outside Helmouth, and the tiger padded in their hearts and at their side.

Seventeen

A full moon had risen over the Black Bone Crags. A perfect ring of light. Stars clustered above the horizons. Cold light fell to the dark green earth over which they walked, Joe, Corinna and the tiger. They headed for the motorway. Sometimes a car's headlights streaked the night there, but they were soon gone, over the northern or the southern horizon. As they walked, they heard noises on the earth and in the air: scratchings, flutterings, short sharp calls and whistles, breath. They heard their own footpads, the swish of grass. At times there was no tiger, but then Joe and Corinna just glanced at each other and walked on, and there it was again, the shimmer of its coat, the glow of its stripes, its breath, its footfall, and its eyes glittering bright as any star. They didn't speak. There was distant yelling and laughter from Helmouth, and Joe thought of his mother there, and her fear, but they didn't turn. They moved through

Joe's familiar places, the lanes and ancient paddocks and ruined streets of what had existed long before. At the far edge of the Field of Skulls, they walked through a broken chain-link fence and climbed up the embankment. They stood on the thin grass by the hard shoulder, stood dead still as a car swept past them. They looked left, looked right, and then ran across the first carriageway. They leaped the crash barrier, and waited again in the central reservation. The tiger stood panting gently. Another car, coming from the north. The great coned beam of its headlights lit them. As it passed, they saw the face of a girl looking out at them, her eyes and mouth wide open as she yelled. The car swerved, slowed, regained its momentum and headed off as quickly as it had come. Joe watched the tail-lights disappear, imagined the voice of the driver: Nonsense. Silly girl. Grow up. Go back to sleep.

They ran again to the other side and down the embankment. Through another ripped fence. They climbed through meadowland towards the Silver Forest. Here the grass was knee-high. Blooms of wild flowers caught the moonlight. The night air was heavy with scents, with pollen. Their breathing deepened as they climbed. They paused, just before the edge of the wood. Joe and Corinna looked at each other in wonder. They looked back towards Helmouth and saw it sparking.

The blue tent softly glowed. The tiger lay in the long grass close by and returned their gaze. Trembling, Joe crouched beside it. He reached out to touch. He laid his hand on the dense fur and felt the tiger's heat, its beating heart. He felt again the beauty and savagery of the tiger in himself. He stood beside the tiger and stared into its eyes. You were in me, he thought. And you came out of me. And you walk beside me in the night. Then Corinna took his hand. They walked on and led the tiger into the Silver Forest.

There was no marked pathway. They walked upwards, between the trunks and stems. There were slender birch trees with flowers and long grass and ferns beneath and alternating shadows and moonlight. There were great beech trees with dry earth beneath and canopy of deepest dark above. Huge oak, their trunks almost as wide as a circus ring. There were stirrings all around. Birds' warning calls. A barn owl screeched. Bodies shifted in the undergrowth, in the shadows. Wings flickered against the stars. The tiger padded onwards, this thing of dream, imagination, truth. It carried ancient scorching grasslands and ancient forests deep into the heart of this English wood.

They came to the stream after an hour or so of walking. It tumbled over mossy stones. Little waterfalls and glinting pools. Moonlight and starlight shimmered in it. They all crouched there, Joe, Corinna and the tiger, and they drank the sweet cold water.

Then the tiger growled, stood up, stared across the stream.

And Joe shuddered, suddenly knowing the awful thing that lay there on the opposite bank.

Eighteen

He stepped across the stones. The body lay curved in the grass. Velvety black. Much smaller than the tiger. The size of a girl, a boy. Joe touched. He watched the shape of his pale hand moving on the black coat. The body was cold and still.

'What is it?' Corinna's voice, coming across the running water. 'Joe. What is it, Joe?'

He ran his fingers through the dense fur. He remembered Stanny's threats and promises. He saw the glint of claws in the panther's feet.

'Joe?'

There was no head, of course. Just congealed blood, a dark stain on the dark grass. He closed his eyes and felt sharpened steel ripping at his throat. He gagged, opened his eyes again.

'Panther,' he whispered.

The tiger watched from over the water, then turned

its head, deeply breathed the night air. Corinna crossed the water. She crouched beside Joe, and shook her head, turned her face to the sky.

'Bastards,' she said, through her tears.

'I know who did it,' said Joe.

The tiger softly growled.

'These people,' she whispered. 'These people you live with!'

She ran her fingers through the black coat.

'Let's find them,' she said.

Her eyes sparkled.

'Let's kill them, Joe. Let's bloody kill them.'

Joe said nothing. He watched the panther. This could have been his own work, if he had come out here carrying knives and hatchets with Stanny Mole and Joff.

The tiger growled again, began to move uphill again. They followed the stream. The crags began to tower over them. The dark peaks were jagged against the sky. Something flew from them on great slow heavy wings. As they walked, they stared into the deep shadows of the trees, looking for the sleeping bodies of their prey. The tiger moved quickly, purposefully, drawing them onwards, through the narrowing gap the stream formed between the trees. Then they caught the scent of fire, saw its embers glowing. It burned in a place where the bank widened, a circle of grass surrounded by tall trees, overlooked by the crags. The moon shone down into this glade.

They stood watching through narrowed eyes. Two bodies lay there in blankets by the fire. Corinna rested her hand on the tiger's shoulder.

'Do you have to believe in the tiger before you can be killed by the tiger?' she said.

'It won't kill them,' said Joe.

'It will. Kill!' she whispered to the tiger. 'Kill!'

It didn't move.

'We could use rocks,' she said. 'Just smash their bloody heads in while they're fast asleep. But mebbe that's too good for them. We could knock them out, then find their bloody knives and saw their heads off like the panther's.'

She spat and cursed in her frustration.

They tiptoed closer. They saw the pile of stones beyond the fire, the panther head set on top of it, the eyes catching the firelight. Corinna gasped. She stroked the tiger.

'Kill them,' she said. 'Go on. Kill them.'

It moved away from them, began to prowl the ring of grass. At times – when it crossed the deepest shadows at the far side, when their eyes failed for a moment to hold it in the world – they lost sight of it. But it kept on reappearing, and when it passed close to them they knew its breath, its scent, and felt the deep disturbance it caused around them in the night.

'Kill,' whispered Corinna. 'Go on. Kill.'

It prowled. It went no closer to the sleeping bodies. It traced circle after circle after circle with the sleeping bodies, the fire and the panther head at the centre. More creatures took wing from the crags above. Shadows shifted at the edges of the glade. The tiger prowled, prowled, its great tail held out behind, its head held high. At times it quickened its step and ran and leaped across the grass, then slowed and walked again. It was always there now, always in view, as if it became more certain of itself, grew more confidently into its new life. The creatures in the sky spiralled downward. Already several were silhouetted in the treetops. Animals stepped out from the forest, half-seen, half-understood things, things half in and half out of the deep darkness: beasts with four legs but with heads that seemed human; beasts that stood erect but with broad horns growing from them; small silvery beasts with single horns; great shaggy beasts as tall as young trees; small shy beasts as short as grass. They gathered there at the fringes in the moonlight. They whispered and whimpered and whinnied. Weird notes and songs escaped from their lips. The creatures high above with their huge beaks and folded wings leaned over and gazed down.

'You see?' hissed Joe.

Corinna trembled.

'You hear?' she said.

The tiger ran. It leaped. It clawed the air. And it began to roar, to hold its head back, open its huge jaws, and roar. And its roars were like something from a deep dark cavern, that filled the glade and echoed round the glade and from the crags.

The sleeping bodies moved.

Joe and Corinna tiptoed closer, dropped to the grass, crawled, waited.

'Kill,' hissed Corinna. 'Kill them!'

Stanny Mole sat up. He rubbed his eyes. He looked around the glade.

'Joff!' he said. 'Joff!'

He shook the man's shoulder. Joff shifted, grunted, snarled.

'Joff!' said Stanny.

The man sat up and cursed. He held his arm against the sky.

'Bloody moon,' he said. 'What the matter with you?'

'Something . . .' said Stanny.

He caught his breath, a sudden short sob or scream. He flinched.

'Joff!' he said.

'Get back to sleep,' the man said. He waved at the air. 'Bloody moon!'

'Oh, God,' said Stanny. 'Oh, my God!'

They saw how his head followed the steps of the tiger now, how he turned to keep it in sight.

'Can you not see?' he said.

'See what?' said the man.

'And there!' said Stanny. 'Oh, and there, and there!'

Joff reached out, grabbed him by the collar.

'It's just the damn panther business,' he said. 'I told you to keep away if you weren't up to it. Calm down, will you? It's just the memory of it.' He turned Stanny's head to the panther head. 'Look, it's bloody dead, boy!'

Stanny shuddered.

'Want to go home!' he sobbed.

He groaned and his arm swung as he pointed to the tiger.

Joff held him then released him.

'Go on, then,' he said. 'Damn kid. Damn stupid kid.'

He shoved Stanny.

'Go on, then, stupid boy.'

Stanny stumbled away from him. He sobbed as the tiger circled him. Joff cursed the moon and dragged the blanket across him.

'You'll soon be back,' he said.

Stanny fell. He found himself staring into the faces of

Joe and Corinna: the trapeze girl, the tiger boy.

'Stanny,' whispered Joe. 'It's me, Stanny.'

He wanted to reach out, touch his friend, comfort him.

'And me,' whispered Corinna. 'Stupid Gyppo fairy tart.'

Stanny swiped his hand across his eyes.

'Oh, God,' he said. 'Oh, my God.'

The tiger prowled.

'It's OK,' said Joe. 'Just run. It won't f-follow.'

'Kill him!' breathed Corinna.

'Just r-run!' said Joe.

Stanny ran, and the beasts parted, and they heard the boy crashing through the undergrowth, through the trees, scrambling downhill.

The tiger was just a few feet from Joff. It held its belly close to the earth. It held its head straight out, level with its shoulders. Its eyes held the man in their grip. It stepped closer, poised to leap.

'Do it, tiger,' said Corinna.

Joe held his breath, waited, watched.

Joff sat up again, held his arm up to the moon, looked into the glade, reached into his blanket, took out a hatchet.

'Who's there?' he hissed.

The tiger growled softly.

'Who's bloody there?'

Rising fear in his harsh voice.

The tiger, low in the grass, crept to him.

'Look how scared he is,' Corinna said. She grinned. 'Look how brave he is. Panther-killer. Do it, tiger!'

She held Joe's hand.

'It won't kill, will it?' she said.

'Don't th-think so.'

Joff held the hatchet shoulder high, backed towards the trees, swung his head as he scanned the glade.

'Bloody moon,' he said. 'Bloody shadows. What's there?'

He beckoned towards himself with his hand, as if he beckoned the glade, the forest, the moon, the night.

'Come on,' he said. 'Show yourself. Come and try it.'

'Lost soul,' sighed Corinna. 'Stupid puny man.'

The tiger closed on him, stood directly before him, so that its breath must fall across him, its scent, the sound of the sighing in its lungs. It growled. But the man saw nothing, heard nothing, smelt nothing. He knew nothing but his own great fear and scorn of what was there before him and all around him. And he started to shudder and gasp and curse like a lost thing. He backed away towards the trees, and again the beasts parted to let him through, and he stumbled away into the forest dark.

Nineteen

Corinna held the head in her hands.

'So beautiful,' she said. 'So heavy. So wonderful. How could they do this?'

They looked into the dark forest that surrounded them. They imagined Stanny and Joff stumbling stupidly through the trees, losing all sense of where they were, losing all sense of who they were. They imagined the creatures of the forest regarding them coldly from their nests and dens and hiding places.

'Stupid man,' said Corinna. 'Stupid, stupid boy.'

She held out the panther head to Joe. He took it into his hands. He felt the dense velvety fur against his palms and fingers. He felt the dried blood and ripped flesh of the awful wound. He gazed down into the empty eyes, imagined the brain behind the eyes, beneath the skull. Was that empty? Nothing in there, ever again? He stared. He dreamed himself into the eyes, into the brain.

He felt the panther dreaming into his own brain, and beginning to run again.

'How could they do this?' Corinna said again.

Joe shook his head.

'Just what people . . . do.'

'People!'

Joe laid the head back on the stones.

'What should we d–do with it?'

'People,' she breathed again. 'People!'

She turned away from Joe. The tiger lay nearby, watching. She stepped towards it, raising her knees high. She held her face to the moon. She stretched her arms out, the fingertips stretched and straining into the night. She cooed and gasped and whimpered. She sang slow intertwining notes. She started to dance in the grass before the tiger.

'Take my hand, Joe.'

He went to her, took her hand, stepped with her, sang with her. They danced around the tiger. They danced in slow circles on the grass.

'People!' she said. 'Forget people, Joe!'

And the other beasts stepped further from the shadows of the forest into the moonlit glade. The shifting and shuffling of their feet and hoofs, the sounds of their weird voices: snuffles and snorts, whistles and gasps, breathy whispers and melodies. The sky was filled with creatures wheeling across the great round moon. The trees and the Black Bone Crags whirled around the glade. The tiger stood and raised its head and roared. Joe and Corinna ran, danced, cartwheeled, moved faster, faster, and they laughed and gasped as they lost themselves in the delight of it. They disappeared and came back again, disappeared and came back again, time and again.

Then slowed and stopped and crouched together at the centre. Looked together at the moon. It paled as the world turned, as day approached again. The creatures stepped back into the trees, flapped back towards the crags. The tiger prowled. Leaves rustled in a pre-dawn breeze.

'It's just like the t-tent,' said Joe.

They looked about them: the walls of crags and trees, fading moon and galaxy above. The tiger. The memory of weird beasts. Two children, hand in hand, dressed in satin, filled with dreams.

Corinna nodded. Yes. It was just like the tent.

'We disappeared,' she said.

'And c-came back again.'

Corinna smiled.

'We'll tell Hackenschmidt. We chased the evil people. We saw the unicorns. We danced with the tiger. We disappeared and came back again. And parts of the world are just like the tent.' She giggled and clapped her hands. 'Parts of the world are just like the tent!'

Joe lifted the panther head.

'What should we do with it, Joe?' she asked.

Joe looked around him.

'We'll hide it,' he said. 'Give it some p-peace.'

They started to walk uphill again, towards the crags.

They looked back. The tiger stayed in the glade, in the grass, watching as they left.

Twenty

At the foot of the crags a small waterfall splashed into a mossy pool. Behind it was a narrow opening in the rock, tall as a boy, a girl. Joe went first. The water sprinkled him. The floor at first was loose wet pebbles then firm dry rock. There was weak light from the entrance, and from weak beams that fell from somewhere high above. The air was icy cold. The space widened and became an echoing empty chamber. Corinna came to Joe's side. The sound of tiny waterdrops, of their breath. Their eyes ached as they accustomed themselves to the light.

'Oh, horses,' whispered Joe.

'Wolves and bears,' said Corinna.

They leaned closer to the rock wall, to the pictures they were sure they saw there. They traced the outlines with their fingers.

'And deer,' whispered Joe.

'Tigers!'

Joe's heart raced. He pointed to the other beasts, winged and horned. The pictures came, merged with the rock, appeared again. And all around they began to make out hand prints, human hand prints. Joe and Corinna searched, found hand prints that fitted their own, and they leaned to the rock like the owners of those prints once had.

They moved further in. Joe held the skull before him, as if the eyes in it might see, might guide them. There was a chest-high shelf in the rock at the far side of the chamber, with a deep dark niche behind. More pictures on the walls, more hand prints. Joe lifted the head and set it on the shelf, and as he did so he felt the other things that were there. He lifted some, held them to his eyes in the semi-dark: bones, fragments of bones, horns, fragments of horns, fangs and teeth. He shuddered as he slid his fingers into the niche. Yet more bones, horns, fangs, teeth. He reached further, reached to arm's length, but the niche stretched beyond his fingertips into total icy dark.

Joe and Corinna stared at each other.

'Like N-Nanty's b—'

'Yes. Like Nanty's box,' said Corinna.

They stared at the panther, into its sightless eyes. They saw the day when the fur had fallen from it, when the flesh and skin were gone, when the eyes were empty sockets, when the brain was gone and there was only the skull of bone and it still rested on the rock shelf and stared into the chamber. They gazed at the rock around themselves, and they saw that the rock was like bone, and that the chamber was like the inside of a skull of bone. And they held their breath as they thought this thought, and felt it moving gently through the soft folds of their brains. Then breathed, and moved backwards across the chamber, bidding farewell to the panther skull.

The scrape of their feet and the sighing of their breath echoed from the walls. They backed out through the narrow passageway, through the sprinkling water. They stood beneath the Black Bone Crags, above the Silver Forest. The world turned and the sun began to show itself above the eastern horizon. From far off came the grumble of the motorway. Joe and Corinna trembled with the delight of being in this place, seeing it, touching it. They trembled with the delight that their minds could think their thoughts, and that they could know such wonder and astonishment.

And the sun rose and the moon faded and the stars went out, and day came back again.

SUNDAY

SUNDAY

One

The tiger was gone. They stood in the glade watching, listening, sniffing the air, but the tiger was gone. Sunlight shone brightly into the glade and shone through leaves and stems into the forest around them. No animals at the forest's edge. No beasts in the air but flitting little birds and larks high up that squealed their lovely songs.

They pulled the blankets and jackets aside and found knives, heavy things with gleaming sharpened blades. They dug a hole with them. They took rocks from the rock pile and pounded the knives till they were broken. They put the broken pieces in the hole. They found a few coins, a tin plate, a whisky bottle, a cigarette lighter. They dropped these into the hole, too, then pushed the earth back in. They kicked the rock pile down. They stirred up the last embers and started a new fire. They put the blankets and the jackets on the fire and stood in the swirling smoke and watched them burn.

'Should be them that's in the fire,' said Corinna, and her eyes darkened as she dreamed the two tormented bodies burning there.

They crouched by the stream as the fire faded. They gulped the water and splashed their faces and rubbed the smoke from their eyes.

'The tiger's going,' said Corinna, touching Joe's face with her fingertips. She showed him the blur of black and white and orange that she wiped away. Joe gulped more water, washed more paint away. Far away, the motorway had begun to drone.

'Let's go,' they whispered, and they looked around themselves again, then left the glade.

Downhill again, through the Silver Forest. The animals they saw were little mice that scuttled for cover as their feet approached, twitching rabbits, spiders dangling on strings or squatting at the centre of their webs, squirrels racing to the tips of swinging branches, worms, black beetles, ants, flies, caterpillars, centipedes. Once a deer stirred and stood in a dense shrub watching them, its dappled skin more dappled by the sun. Once a snake uncoiled itself and slithered from the mossy bank where it had basked in the light. Joe and Corinna picked their way between the trees, stepped across fallen branches, across ferns and toadstools, over pools of water, through boggy turf, through knee-high grass. They passed the bank where the panther's body lay. Already the flies and worms were at their work, and had begun to strip the body to its bone. They stood over it in silence for a time and wished it peace, then walked on through sun and shade, through the brackish scents of the forest, towards the noise of the motorway, towards the tent and Helmouth and home. And their thoughts moved from what they'd known in the night towards what they might find waiting in the day. And they quickened their step, wanting to be home again, wanting to move on. The world kept on turning, the sun kept on rising. They became warm and they smiled at each other as they wiped the sweat from their brows. They smiled more deeply at the thought that they had found each other, that they were friends, twins, that they would stay close to each other now, that a new life had started for them. Sometimes they laughed as they walked and just exclaimed each other's name.

'Joe Maloney!'

'Corinna Finch!'

'Joe!'

'Corinna!'

'Oh!'

'Ah!'

'Ha!'

'Ha! Ha! Ha!'

They smiled more quietly when the tiger came. It moved at a distance through the forest shade. It moved with them, step by step. Soon they approached the forest's edge. They caught glimpses of the meadow, of the motorway. Soon they stepped through the edge and stood together in knee-high grass and bright red poppies with a breeze blowing on them and the sunlight falling full on them. The tiger stayed inside. They saw its gleaming eyes, saw its stripes merging with the sun and shade, saw its mouth open in a final roar of farewell. Then it turned and moved back into the forest, and disappeared there.

'Goodbye,' Joe whispered.

Then closed his eyes, felt the tiger prowling through the forest of his mind, knew the tiger would prowl in him for ever more.

Two

'Run!' yelled Corinna.

There was a gap in the traffic but a huge car transporter and a silver Mercedes thundered towards them as they sprinted over the carriageway. There was the squeal of brakes and blast of a great horn as they leaped into the safety of the central reservation. Traffic roared past them. Drivers yelled and shook their fists. Faces gaped in fear or amazement.

'Now!' yelled Corinna, and they ran again and flung themselves on to the hard shoulder and on to the far embankment and they rolled downhill to the broken fence and lay there gasping and laughing. And picked themselves up and headed through the Ratty Paddocks with the breeze at their backs towards home.

Stanny Mole crouched on the floor of the Blessed Chapel. Raised his head as Joe and Corinna approached. Watched them in silence, then:

'You seen Joff?'

Joe shook his head.

'He's not come down yet,' said Stanny.

'He'll be lost,' said Corinna, and she gave the boy a cold stare. 'Or worse,' she said.

Stanny blinked, turned his face away from her, and Joe saw how his friend was filled with questions, heard how the words to ask them were tangled and twisted on his tongue.

'What . . .?' Stanny stammered. 'W-why?'

Joe looked towards the village. Kids in uniform were making their way towards Hangar's High. He shrugged, didn't know how to answer. Stanny watched him for a while, then hung his head. Tears dripped from his eyes.

'I hurt me hand, look, Joe,' he said.

He showed his right hand, a bloody gash across the palm. Joe took it in his own hand, touched the blood with his fingertip.

'I saw . . .' said Stanny. 'I thought I saw . . .'

He cried again.

'Poor boy,' whispered Corinna. 'If I had a knife . . .'

Joe turned his back to her.

'Leave him,' he said softly.

'It wasn't me,' Stanny said. 'Wasn't me. I know I said I wanted to do it but once we started I didn't want to do it, but I wanted to see it and watch him and . . .'

He sobbed, sucking in sudden breaths, coughing them out again. He rocked on the floor of the chapel and the breeze blew over him and whistled in the stones.

Corinna spat.

'Poor poor boy,' she breathed. 'Such a shame for you.'

Then she quietened, as the two boys crouched in the Blessed Chapel reflecting on their friendship and the panther's death.

'There was blood all over,' said Stanny. 'Splashing all over . . . On my hands, on the grass . . .'

He stared at Joe.

'And the sound of the knife, and the . . .'

He shuddered.

'Then last night . . . like a dream, but . . .'

'Not a dream,' said Joe.

'Joe,' said Corinna. 'Come on.'

She tugged gently at Joe's sleeve.

'What do you do,' said Stanny, 'when you've done something you said you wanted to do but you didn't want to do but you've done it anyway and you can't undo it and . . .?'

He shuddered into silence. He looked towards the motorway, the Silver Forest, the Black Bone Crags, then back to Joe again.

'Too late for anything,' said Corinna. 'It's done. You're

evil and you'll always be evil. Ah, poor soul. Come on, Joe.'

'I was your friend, Joe,' said Stanny Mole.

Joe wiped the wound on Stanny's hand with moist moss. He pressed Stanny's hand on to the broken stones, wiped it across the name of God.

'Sp-spirits of the earth and air, look after Stanny Mole this day.'

He touched soil to Stanny's tongue. He snapped a button from Stanny's shirt and dropped it into the space between the stones.

'So what will you do now?' said Corinna.

She stood with her arms folded, looking down at them.

'D-do?' said Stanny.

'To make up for it, you fool.'

He blinked, and wiped his cheeks. He looked at Joe.

Corinna laughed. She pointed at Stanny.

'You must repeat the name of the panther one hundred times every dawn and every dusk. You must fast every Friday for the next six weeks. You must . . .'

Stanny turned his face from her.

'You'll be my friend?' he said.

'Yes,' said Joe. 'I'll be your f-friend.'

Corinna tugged at his sleeve. He stepped from the floor, across the collapsed walls and broken stones of the chapel. Corinna stepped lightly at his side.

'Bring things to life, Stanny Mole,' she called over her shoulder. 'Don't do them to death.'

Three

The sun strengthened and the light above the wasteland trembled. The faded blueness of the tent matched the blueness of the sky. It shimmered in the sun and shivered in the breeze. The guy-ropes creaked. The summit gently swayed. A poster saying **LAST DAY** drifted slowly across the slope of the tent and was carried away towards Helmouth. The billboards of the animals and of Hackenschmidt rocked. Caravans were already moving off, trundling across the rough ground, pulled by lurching cars.

Someone yelled, 'Good riddance, scum! And don't come back!'

A stone clanked across the bonnet of an ancient Austin.

Someone howled, 'Only Maloney, lalalala!'

Someone screamed, 'Stupid Gyppo fairy tart!'

But they took no notice, didn't even turn.

Charley Caruso called, 'Tomasso! Tomasso! Tomasso!

Tomasso!' far off and frail and so filled with yearning.

'What shall we do?' said Corinna.

'D-do?'

'With our lives. What shall we do? Where shall we go?'

Joe laughed.

'We can d-do anything! We can g-go anywhere! Look!'

She knelt and picked something from the grass. A broken skylark shell, speckled white. Joe touched. The curved inside was dry, but sticky on his fingertip. He dreamed of the thing that had been in there, white and yolk that had turned to bone and flesh and feather, the thing that had bitten its way out, that had dared to fling itself into the air. He looked into Corinna's face, speckled white. He looked through to the forests and crags and caves and skies behind her eyes. And their faces turned together to the air, where a storm of larks danced high on the wind and sang.

'Miracle,' said Joe.

'Miracle,' said Corinna.

They moved on. She lifted the flap of the tent and they stepped through into the silent sombre shade and found Hackenschmidt and Nanty Solo there, sitting together on the low wall at the ring's edge.

Nanty raised her milky eyes. She smiled.

'So our little loved ones flutter home again,' she said. 'Welcome home, little loved ones.'

Hackenschmidt came to them and hugged them both to his great chest.

'It went well,' he said.

Corinna nodded.

'And the tiger's gone.'

'The tiger's gone.'

He cradled Joe's head in his great fist.

'You have done a great thing, Joe Maloney. You have done a thing that is filled with courage and that is beyond our understanding.' He stared deeper. 'How did we find a boy like you in a place like Helmouth?'

'Was destined,' said Corinna.

'Yes,' answered Hackenschmidt. 'It was destined, from the time the tent first stood upon the earth.'

'We followed you,' said Nanty Solo. 'Far as the forest.' She tapped her skull. 'In here,' she said.

'And did you see the glade and the . . .?' said Corinna, but Nanty pressed her crooked finger to Corinna's lips.

'Don't,' she said. 'You must keep your secret places for yourselves.'

And she drew Corinna to her and kissed her and the tent around them trembled.

'We been talking and dreaming 'bout the old days,' said Nanty. ''Bout the old days when the canvas was so new that it blocked out all the light. Now you see it thin and frayed and it carries a million million points of light upon it. Soon the rips and lesions will start, and the wind will play at these till they open further and great shafts of light will fall into this place. And the wind will keep on playing and rampaging till the rips race everywhere and the tent will give its final shivers and collapse. Then there will be nothing but emptiness above this place, just as there was all that time back, the time there was no tent at all.'

She laughed softly.

'And we been talking 'bout what happens to the ancient crazy blind one and the ancient wrestler in these new days, and Nanty looks and looks inside her skull and can see nothing there for them at all.'

She raised her head.

'Come on down, tent. Fall down and cover us and let us be still beneath. Come on down!'

She shrugged, smiled.

'Ah, well. It'll come, in its own time.'

Corinna laughed.

'Come on up,' she said to Joe, and she took his hand.

She went first up the dangling ladder. She clambered through the net. She stood on the platform. Joe followed, climbing away from the two old ones below. He stood on the platform beside his friend.

'Imagine,' she said. 'Imagine that once upon a time you flew out there, swinging back and forwards, waiting for me to leap. Can you imagine that?'

'Yes.'

'Really imagine it?'

'Yes.'

'Imagine it so strong it's nearly like a memory and not just like a dream?'

'Yes.'

'And imagine I jumped and you caught me and we swung out there together and the crowd gasped at how wonderful we were?'

'Yes. Yes.'

'And so strong it's more like a memory than a dream?'

'Yes.'

She laughed.

'We were together, Joe, you and me. Sometime long ago, in another world or in another life. We flew together. Do you believe that?'

'Yes. Yes.'

'Jump!' called Hackenschmidt.

'Jump!' whispered Corinna, and hand in hand they leaped into the empty air, through memories and dreams, through other worlds and other lives, and the net sighed as it caught them in this world, in this life and kept them safe.

Four

A pot-bellied pig named Fatty. Little dogs in silver dresses teetering on hind legs. Good Wilfred in his goatee beard and Charley Caruso with his mind lost in the past. They all came into the tent as Joe and Corinna dropped down to the floor again. They gathered in the ring, so pleased to see the children back.

Then another, her face at the doorway peering in.

'Joe!' she called. 'Joseph!'

'Mum!'

'There you are!'

She came quickly across the floor and hugged him. She grinned.

'Hello, Corinna, pet. He's behaved himself?'

'Yes,' said Corinna.

'Good lad.'

'This is Hackenschmidt,' said Corinna. 'He's the owner of the circus. This is Nanty Solo. This is Wilfred.

This is Charley Caruso. This is Joe's mum.'

She beamed at them all and hugged Joe again.

'It is a delight to meet you, madam,' said Wilfred. 'You are indeed blessed to have such a son.'

'There's many that'd doubt that, Wilfred, but aye, it's the truth. Look at the skill of that dog! You had breakfast, Joseph?'

Joe's stomach growled. He shook his head.

'I'm f—'

'Famished, eh? Come on, then. Let's get something on the table.'

'I want to bring my fr-friends.'

'That's great. If you'd like to, that is . . . It's a little house, Mr Hackenschmidt. We might have to spill out into the garden.'

Hackenschmidt grinned.

'It will be a pleasure, Mrs Maloney.'

She looked around herself before she led them out.

'Oh, isn't it so beautiful in here?' she said.

And she stood lost in that beauty and the silence of it for a moment, before she led the way out.

This motley crew came from the blue tent on to the rough wasteland of Helmouth. They moved slowly, contentedly, beneath the high slow sun. The pig snuffled in the undergrowth. The dogs danced. Nanty Solo held the arm of Hackenschmidt and told tales of long ago.

Good Wilfred walked daintily with his head high, whistling and calling to his dogs, and whispering gentle guidance into Charley Caruso's ear. Joe and Corinna in their satins strolled on either side of Joe's mum.

'Come on, then. What did you get up to?' she said.

'Went on the tr-trapeze.'

'The trapeze! And no broken bones!'

'And played in the tent,' said Corinna. 'And played with the dogs and . . .'

'And the tigers didn't eat you up?'

Joe smiled.

'There's n-no tigers,' he said.

'No tigers! So what was them things jumping and growling in my head all night. Like a blinking zoo, my bedroom was.'

'Just dreams,' he said.

'Mebbe,' she said.

'Aye. Mebbe.'

He looked at her and smiled. She hugged him. He leaned into her, towards the great spaces where her larks flew and her wild beasts prowled.

'It's lovely to have you back. You know, Corinna, that's the first full night we've ever spent apart.'

He grinned as she kissed him.

'You're growing up, Joseph Maloney. You know that, don't you?'

'Yes.'

'Seems no time since you were crawling round me feet, and look at you now. And you, Corinna. You must've been a lovely lively bairn, eh? Dancing and jumping and swinging everywhere, I'll bet.'

'That's right, Mrs Maloney.'

'Oh, just look at these louts!'

Kids clustered around the entrance to the Cut, cigarettes cupped in their fists, grins on their faces, hell in their eyes.

'Come on,' Joe's mum said. 'Clear the way, will you?'

'Yes, Missus Maloney. Of course, Missus Maloney. Only Maloney, lalalalaaaaaaa!'

'Here comes the beast!'

'Watch out! Wild dogs!'

'Run! It's the Pig of Death!'

'Keep out, scum!'

'Keep out, scum! Keep out, scum!'

They beckoned to Hackenschmidt, they spat at Corinna, they snarled at Nanty, they sneered at Charley and Wilfred.

'Look at them. Turn the place into a bloody loony bin.'

'A freak show!'

'Tarts and witches and poofs and pigs.'

'Fat and blind and doo-lally!'

But they kept their distance. Wonder and fear were in their eyes as well as scorn. They parted slowly as the group passed through.

'Poor souls,' whispered Nanty into Joe's ear. 'Poor troubled souls.'

'Get lost, scum!'

'Keep out, scum!'

'Get back to where you come from!'

'Only Maloney, lalalalaaaaaa!'

Beyond them, younger children waited on the pavement in the estate. They caught at each other's hands as they saw the group approach. Their eyes were wide, fascinated. They whispered Joe Maloney's name. They gasped at the bulk of famous Hackenschmidt. They giggled at the dancing dogs. They cooed at the sweet slow pig. They trembled as they reached out to touch these folk. And there were faces at the windows, suspicious faces, faces filled with hate, but also faces shining with delight.

Joe's mum led them on.

'It's that house,' she said, and pondered. 'It's nothing, look. Little, just ordinary. But there's the garden, too, to sit in. And there's tea and coffee and bread to fill us all and marmalade. And jam. Oh, and some lovely sausages, and an egg or two. A bunch of bananas. That punnet of rasps. A feast! And there's surely scraps for the dogs, and what does the pig eat, Mr Hackenschmidt? Come on. Come on in.'

In they went through the low garden gate, past the little wilderness of weeds and wild flowers where Joe once played. She led them to the back of the house, to the little back garden, fumbled in her pocket for her keys.

'Anybody need the loo?' she said softly. 'Top of the stairs, straight left.' She chewed her lips, her eyes shone: such strange animals, such strange sweet people here in her garden. 'Ee, Joseph, it's just like those tales you used to jabber come to life. Now, who's for coffee, who's for tea? Joe, get those thirsting dogs a dish of water, son.'

Five

They sat at ease in the garden, on the rugs and blankets that Joe's mum brought out of the house. They ate pieces of sausage, fruit and toast. They praised the deliciousness of the food, the beauty of the garden, the kindness of Mrs Maloney. They murmured softly to each other, they hummed songs, they sighed, they smiled. Helmouth's children peered from the front gate. Neighbours leaned out from the windows. The sun poured down through the skylarks' endless song.

Corinna left the ground and skipped in a circle, then turned cartwheels, and everybody clapped. She stared upwards, as if searching for a trapeze and a net. She closed her eyes and allowed the heat and brightness to bathe her, then she spun again and dropped to the earth again.

And they rested, as afternoon came on, all of them exhausted by their sleepless night. They drifted and dozed. Joe rested his head in his mum's lap. She ran her fingers through his hair. Joe dipped his hands into long grass and smiled at the spiders and beetles that ran on his skin and he closed his eyes.

A couple of children, a boy and a girl, dared to come closer. They sidled down the path at the side of the house. They sat on their haunches and whispered and watched. The girl held out her hand, rubbed her fingers together to catch the attention of the dogs. And one skipped to her and licked her and she laughed.

Mrs Maloney opened her eyes.

'Come in, pets,' she said. 'Come on. Look, there's some bits of toast here.'

And they came shyly into the garden and Nanty Solo smiled behind her milky eyes and Corinna stood up and spun again around the circle of grass that was clear at the centre of the garden.

'That was lovely,' said the girl.

More children came, to play with the dogs and the pig, to watch Corinna.

'I brought this,' said a green-eyed girl with eagles on her T-shirt. She held out a long linked string of elastic bands. 'Show us what to do again.'

They stretched the elastic right across the garden from fence to fence. Corinna showed them how to leap with ease and grace. She raised the elastic higher. She showed them how to leap as if they believed that they might leap as high as the sun.

'Jump!' said Hackenschmidt. 'Jump. Don't just jump with your bodies. Jump with your minds.'

'Jump through the sunlight,' said Nanty Solo. 'Close your eyes and jump into the dark.'

'J–jump,' said Joe Maloney. 'D–dare to fling yourself into the empty air.'

His mum smiled.

'Joe Maloney,' she whispered, 'look at you now. Listen to you now.'

And the children in the garden jumped and fell and tried again and jumped again and Corinna jumped with them, time and again.

Nanty whispered, 'On the last day, on the last of all days . . .'

She turned her head as if she looked around her. She smiled to herself.

'The last of all days is mebbe when we find the first of all days. Jump, children, jump!'

Cats came, looking out from beneath the hedges. Birds gathered on rooftops and gutters. Bees droned from flower-head to flower-head. A tiny mouse peeped out from a clump of buttercups.

Joe's mum held him tight.

Soon Stanny Mole came down the path beside the house. He shuffled into the garden. He squatted near to Joe and trembled.

'He's not come out yet,' he whispered.

Joe closed his eyes and saw through the tiger's eyes and saw Joff stumbling through trees, all lost and tormented.

'They'll k-kill him,' said Stanny. 'Those . . . things we saw.'

'No. He'll c-come back,' said Joe. He touched his friend's arm. He wondered what changes would be wrought in Joff by his struggle in the forest.

Nanty Solo stretched to Stanny, her hand held out, a black fragment in her fingers.

'Eat this, boy-thing,' she said.

Stanny recoiled.

'Eat,' she said.

'What is it?'

'Eat.'

Stanny looked in horror at her milky eyes, her scar.

'Eat,' said Joe. 'Just eat.'

Stanny opened his mouth, allowed her to rest the thing on his tongue.

'Eat, Stanny Mole,' said Nanty. 'Just eat.'

He swallowed. Nanty put her fingers to her lips.

'Be quiet,' she said. 'Be still. And feel the tooth of the

unicorn at work inside yourself. For all of us can be transformed.'

And Stanny was quiet and all that was heard was the snuffling of the pig, the hum of the bees, the distant din of the city, the drone of the motorway.

Then Wilfred took his turn and his little dogs danced for him as he whistled and called. Then Hackenschmidt asked two boys to come to him and he showed them how to be still and show no fear as he lifted them, one in each hand, high above his head. And he laughed and roared and shouted,

'Listen! I am Hackenschmidt. I am the greatest wrestler the world has ever seen. All I say is true! Who dares to challenge me and win a thousand pounds?'

He beat his chest and snarled and laughed as boys ran at him and circled him.

All quietened again and the children looked at each other in fear and wonder and the afternoon wore on. The sun arched downwards, filling the garden with light and heat, stunning all who were inside it. The air trembled. Beyond the rooftops, the beautiful blue slope of the tent slanted into the sky.

And the afternoon wore on, and the afternoon wore on, and shadows lengthened.

Mothers started calling, their voices echoing through Helmouth, over the rooftops, through the gardens.

'Dani–eeeeeel!'

'Em–i–leeeeeee!'

'Ma–aaax!'

And children stirred themselves, and rubbed their eyes and stretched themselves and made their way back out of Joe Maloney's garden.

Corinna leaped and spun again for the few children who were left. Wilfred danced his dogs again. Hackenschmidt murmured,

'I am Hackenschmidt, Lion of Russia, greatest wrestler the world has ever seen.'

He turned to his tent, saw that it had blended with the sky, had almost disappeared in the coming night.

'Hackenschmidt. Come and sit by me,' said Nanty Solo, and he sat by her. 'Come and wait for the first day to come again.'

Inside the shadows, there were creatures in the wild long grass. They were shadows, shifting shapes, mice and beetles, and other half-seen things, half-known things. Joe stared and his mum stared and they thought of Joe's pictures in the house, those pictures from so long ago. And Stanny Mole stared too, and crawled across the grass to Joe and sat by his friend.

'And you?' said Nanty Solo, reaching out to Joe. 'What will you do, Joe Maloney, here in the garden?'

Joe blushed, looked away, chewed his lips. The

children who were left giggled. For they knew Joe. They knew Only Maloney.

'Come on,' said Hackenschmidt. 'Come on, Joe Maloney. Bring the last day to an end.'

'Do it, Joe,' whispered Corinna. 'Refresh the world.'

Joe lowered his head, so shy again. A pale moon appeared over the Black Bone Crags. First stars were out. The garden was like the tent. Joe closed his eyes and heard the tiger padding through the forest. It stepped from the forest's edge, as if in answer to his call. It quickened as it crossed the wasteland. He heard the breath, the heart. Joe stood, and he walked with the tiger inside him. He prowled, he clawed the air, he leaped. And the children laughed at this but then they quietened for they began to hear the tiger, here in this Helmouth garden. They heard its footsteps and its breath. They caught the sour scent of it. They felt the disturbance in the air around them. They saw it move across the edges of their vision, and they turned their heads in fear and fascination, trying to follow it, trying to catch sight again of the stripes, the glittering eyes, the curved teeth of the fearful thing that walked before them with Joe Maloney. Then Joe became still. He sat with his mum again.

She started to sing:

'If I were a little bird, high up in the sky,
This is how I'd flap my wings and fly, fly, fly.
If I were a cat . . .'

She smiled.

'We'll find a lovely life, Joe, you and me, tomorrow
when the sun comes back.'

'And all of us,' said Nanty Solo.

Joe nodded.

'Yes,' he said. 'All of us.'

He leaned on his mum. He gazed into Corinna's
dark eyes. With everyone in the garden, he began to
sleep. The world beneath them turned towards the day.
The tiger crossed the wasteland. It padded back towards
the forest through the night.